THE WILDE KINGDOM

"Is there anyone special in your life?"

"Special? No. At this time in my life, my career is everything." The warmth of Eli's hand on her cheek was distracting Chloe. "I never thought it'd be fair to subject anyone to my erratic schedule or my moods."

"Not fair?" Eli stroked his thumb back and forth over Chloe's lower lip. "I'll probably get to see my fair share of your moods during the next three months. I'm beginning to look forward to every one of them." He brought his thumb up to trace her cheekbone. "I'm a little concerned, to be honest, about how you'll react to *my* moods."

"Are you temperamental?" She heard a rasp in her own voice and knew it echoed the desires his touch was stirring.

"Terribly."

"I thought you said recluses weren't antisocial?"

"As a group, we're generally misunderstood."

"You're making me laugh intentionally, Eli. I don't know why—but I feel so good tonight."

Eli pulled her closer, his hand a firm pressure that moved down to the base of her spine. "I'm glad to hear you're feeling good." His mouth hovered over hers. "You'll feel even better . . . when I kiss you."

Jamisan Whitney

After more than a decade of juggling concurrent careers as a freelance photographer and a television writer/producer, Jamisan Whitney began writing romantic fiction full time.

Jamisan is currently settled in Seattle where she enjoys watching sunsets with her husband, Jerry "J. C." Chan, who works in broadcasting.

Jamisan is the first recipient of Romantic Times' Wish Award, presented to contemporary authors for portrayals of a memorable hero. She is also published under her real name, Noreen Brownlie.

Other Second Chance at Love books by Jamisan Whitney

DRIVEN TO DISTRACTION #315
HEAVEN SENT #423
DESTINY'S DESIRE #431

Dear Reader:

After many wonderful years filled with some of the best romance novels to be offered, Second Chance at Love will be publishing its final titles next month. To be sure, this was a difficult decision to make. Since its inception, Second Chance at Love has been lauded for providing consistently enjoyable love stories month after month. Thousands of you—from many countries—have told us how pleased you've been. We'd like to thank you again for making Second Chance at Love a product of affection and success to the very end.

Now for this month's books...

From the author of *Absolute Beginners* comes *Sugar & Cinnamon* (#474). Jack McMillan is a professional stuntman between jobs. It's a good thing, too, because he's mysteriously summoned by the mysterious will of a woman he's never heard of—to a small town in the middle of nowhere. Jack couldn't be happier. Never one to sit still for long, he packs up his convertible, prepared to take his claim. He's only been there hours when he realizes there's more than just an inheritance awaiting him. There's Sophie Parrish, the difference between a twist of fate and divine destiny. A young widowed mother of twin baby girls, Sophie's life boasts very little excitement and absolutely no surprises. It's only when she meets Jack and gets to know him better that she realizes just how miraculous life can be. Certain that happiness like this can be only temporary, Sophie provides Jack with a graceful out. Happily for Jack, he comes up with a very pleasurable contradiction ...Courtney Ryan at her best is *Sugar & Cinnamon*.

In *The Wilde Kingdom* (#475) by Jamisan Whitney, world-class cartoonist Chloe Wilde, usually a carefree and creative spirit, has been struck by a monumental case of burnout. Panicked and desperate for inspiration, Chloe sets out for Eli Kellerman's highly touted country hideaway. An artist of another sort, Eli not only understands Chloe's predicament, he seems to know just how to make it better. Along with numerous mutual interests, they begin to share an intimacy each has always longed for. And then a strange thing happens. Both media darlings, sought-after celebrities accustomed to being in the spotlight, Eli and Chloe begin to wonder if they've fallen in love with perfected images or the real thing...

Determination and trust pull together to help *true* love win in the end.

Also from Berkley this month...

It's New Orleans, 1941. The oil boom that brought two decades of limitless wealth and luxury to this sultry city draws to a close as the clouds of war loom on the horizon. This is the sweeping epic of *To Love and To Dream* by acclaimed author Elizabeth Nell Dubus. Now even the Langlinais, who had always known money, power, and privilege, must remake their lives—and their name—in the tumultuous dawn of World War II. For Skye Langlinais and his beautiful stepsister, Caro, the passion of war brings with it the passion of human emotions—and a world of broken promises. Together they rush headlong into uncertain destinies, determined to start anew. For though their honor has been stolen, nothing can stop their hearts from dreaming...

Bestselling author Roberta Gellis called *A Different Eden* by new author Katherine Sinclair "fast-moving and exciting." Laurie McBain found it "touching" and "absorbing." Katherine's newest, *Visions of Tomorrow,* is all that and more. In the grand tradition of Janet Dailey's *Calder* series, Ms. Sinclair paints a glorious picture of two women who share the wonder and promise of a twentieth-century that's just a heartbeat away...Megan and Joanna were lifelong friends—until a night of tragedy tore them apart—and sent them on two separate journeys of the heart. They're thrown into new and changing worlds, from turn-of-the-century Cornwall to the rugged frontiers of New Mexico to the bustling excitement of New York, where they will challenge the future and shape their own fates. This is an absolutely riveting read. Don't miss it.

As always, enjoy and...happy reading!

Hillary Cige

Hillary Cige, Editor
SECOND CHANCE AT LOVE
The Berkley Publishing Group
200 Madison Avenue
New York, NY 10016

JAMISAN WHITNEY
THE WILDE KINGDOM

BERKLEY BOOKS, NEW YORK

THE WILDE KINGDOM

Copyright © 1989 by Noreen Brownlie

All rights reserved. No part of this publication may be reproduced or transmitted in any form or by any means, electronic or mechanical, including photocopy, recording, or any information storage and retrieval system, without permission in writing from the publisher.

Requests for permission to make copies of any part of the work should be mailed to: Permissions, Second Chance at Love, The Berkley Publishing Group, 200 Madison Avenue, New York, NY 10016.

First edition published November 1989

ISBN: 0-425-11842-8

"Second Chance at Love" and the butterfly emblem are trademarks belonging to Jove Publications, Inc. The name "BERKLEY" and the "B" logo are trademarks belonging to Berkley Publishing Corporation.

Second Chance at Love books are published by
The Berkley Publishing Group
200 Madison Avenue, New York, NY 10016

Printed in the United States of America

10 9 8 7 6 5 4 3 2 1

Dedicated with love and appreciation

to my friends and fellow authors Stella Cameron, Jayne Ann Krentz, Debbie Macomber, and Linda Lael Miller

Chapter 1

BAR-B-CUE WOULD HAVE loved this party. Chloe Wilde locked the bedroom door behind her and the familiar black-and-white image focused in her mind. With bovine abandon, her cartoon creation would kick up those famous painted Holstein hooves and dance with Seattle's elite. The doers. The shakers. The movers. In the case of Bar-B-Cue the Cow, it would be *mooers*.

Chloe's whimsical thoughts faded. Party music, loud conversation, and laughter filtered through the locked door, feeding the warm tide of frustration that had been welling in her veins all evening. Her future was in jeopardy and, as usual, her mind was filled with animal imagery. The problem was getting the pictures from her brain to the paper.

Chloe crossed the room and rested her fingers atop

the phone on the dimly lit bedside table. This was an emergency—of sorts. She had to call someone for help. But who?

Every person she considered a friend was here, celebrating—while she deliberated in her hosts' bedroom. Chloe glanced back toward the door. The two inches of ornately carved wood were probably the thinnest of barriers that stood between her and these fifty-odd intimate strangers. What person among them would understand her crisis, and, more importantly, how long would they be willing to withhold the news from the press? She'd been betrayed too many times in the past.

She needed advice, preferably from someone who knew nothing about her public image. After lifting the Seattle phone book off a lower shelf, Chloe sat down on the bed. The tissue-thin pages stuck to her moist fingertips, slowing her search. She swallowed hard as she dabbed the palms of both hands against the ruffled skirt of her strapless party dress.

She scanned the community service numbers for hotlines. Alcohol, drugs, medical, legal, domestic violence, senior citizens' information, women's rights, mental health. The muted pages resting on her lap were a sharp contrast to the vibrant purple taffeta of her short skirt.

The reality and the fantasy, she thought with a self-mocking smile, as she ran one of her nails, painted in "Violet Nights" for the occasion, over the listings a second time. TRAVELER'S AID. Her gaze rested on the bold type. There was a phone number for almost every concern. Why wasn't there a hotline for burned-out cartoonists?

Her early life had been a succession of dark clouds and crises. Searching for silver linings had been her challenge. One of those elusive linings had actually turned to gold and then quickly to platinum. Now she needed strength to deal with the fact that her glittering career was finished.

She'd ignored the warning signs for two months: the bouts of lethargy, the self-doubt, the loss of inspiration. And then this morning—what was left of Chloe Wilde, one of America's most celebrated female cartoonists, couldn't even pick up her sketching pen?

With a burst of impatience, Chloe shoved the phone book off her lap and pushed a series of buttons on her hosts' telephone. The taffeta rustled as she fell back across the bed, counting the rings aloud.

". . . eight, nine, ten—"

"H-hello?" A sleepy male voice answered.

"Marty, it's me . . . Chlo-ee." Her confidence faltered. Was she pulling some prima donna act, calling her business manager in the middle of the night? "I know it's late—"

"No problem." The sound of Marty's fist punching a pillow failed to disguise the muffled curse that followed. "My phone's always open to you. Is everything all right? Sorry I couldn't make the party. Did you get my birthday present?"

Chloe recalled the exquisite silver pendant. "The elephant was beautiful. You shouldn't have, but thank you. I appreciate it." She searched for the words to explain her dilemma and felt a wave of apprehension at the thought of hurting this gentle man.

"Marty—it stopped completely this morning. I'm afraid it's over."

"Don't be so cryptic, Chloe. *What* stopped?"

"The inspiration, the characters, my career. I woke up this morning, tried to draw a strip, and nothing happened. Nothing."

"Hey, hey, stay calm," Marty interrupted. "There's a simple explanation here. I'm sorry you're going through this, but we'll figure it out. Maybe you've gotten yourself worked up over turning thirty. All artists and writers have temporary blocks."

There was silence for a moment.

"Chloe, I hear music and voices. It's three in the morning. You're still at the party?"

"It's not a school night," she chided.

"Jeez. You didn't mention this creative block to Gregory and Louise, did you?" Martin Blashfield was on full alert now. Chloe could hear the strain in the older man's voice.

Gregory and Louise Waters were hosting the party. They owned a chain of stationery boutiques that carried "The Wilde Kingdom" line of cards. Chloe's line.

"I haven't told anyone about my problem, Marty, and I'm not dumb enough to breathe a word of it to the Waterses."

"Good. Maybe you should go circulate a bit. After all, you're the guest of honor."

"I don't really feel close to these people. I'm not sure if they like the real me or the mystique that's been hyped by the media." Still lying across the bed, Chloe pointed her toes forward. Her designer heels slipped to the floor, hitting the plush carpet with two unsatisfying thuds.

"Ch-looo-eeee." Marty turned the two syllables into three with a yawn. "All this sudden success is catching up with you. Keep yourself grounded and remember everything you've got going for you. Talent, a place on the best-seller list, financial security, and your extraordinary looks. Your face has been on more than a dozen covers in the past two months alone. Why don't you pick up a magazine? There must be magazines there. Have you ever stopped to count your—"

Only half listening to the sound of Marty's voice, Chloe sat up and searched through the stack of magazines on top of the bedside table until she found a dog-eared copy of *Sublime*. A kinky-haired woman with dark oblique eyes and a generous mouth clowned on the cover. She opened the slick pages to the lead story, recalling her reaction to the insipid article and accompanying photographs.

"Marty, shall I read aloud from the latest issue of *Sublime*?" she asked, then proceeded without waiting for a reply. " 'Ms. Wilde's eyes have a sleepy, languid visage about them, a gift from her Moroccan father. Even when smiling, her lips possess a sweetly ravaged puffiness . . . an eternal pout.' "

Marty sighed. "I know it's a bit sexist but that

magazine practically sold out. I have clients who would kill for the coverage you're getting. You're approaching the zenith of your career, Chloe. You're syndicated in over seven hundred newspapers and then there's the—"

"Bedroom eyes and ravaged lips? What kinds of insults should I expect when I *reach* my zenith? I want to be viewed as a professional, but everyone insists on perpetuating this image of *Chloe, the sex symbol of cartooning*. I trust you to take this matter and the problem of my artistic block seriously, Marty. I'm in the middle of a crisis!"

"What do you want me to do? Call your publicist and arrange a press conference?"

"Yes!" Chloe replied without hesitation. She didn't care about deadlines or contracts anymore. This time she felt like pleasing only one person. Herself. Standing up, she slipped her feet back into the silver heels. "The truth is simple. I need to take a sabbatical. You're my business manager and I want the announcement handled in a professional manner."

"A sabbatical? And what are you going to tell your adoring public?" The first hint of annoyance rippled through Marty's well-spaced words.

"We'll tell them the truth. I've lost my inspiration. The workload is too heavy. The deadlines, the publicity, the advertising contracts—it's too much. I need to get away for a couple of months and sort things out. After five years, a vacation isn't too much to ask." Chloe hated the pleading edge she heard in her own voice. Why should she have to beg?

"And just where do you plan to go where people won't know your face?" Marty's tone softened.

Chloe glanced down at the cover of *Sublime*. She felt an odd elation. "Somewhere very green and remote, someplace quiet, where no one knows anything about me."

"That's easy. We'll just send you to the moon—the grassy side, of course. Be serious, sweetheart. I'm tryin' to help you."

"I've never taken a sabbatical before, Marty." Chloe stepped toward the window. "I thought *you* knew about these things."

Marty spoke after a long silence. "Hmmm, maybe I do. I remember some friends of mine telling me about a new artist who just returned from the West Coast. The guy rented a cottage from that sculptor that's getting so much press—Kellerman, Eli Kellerman. This Kellerman's got a farmhouse and acreage on the Olympic Peninsula in Washington State. Nice lush scenery with a guest cottage close by. He rents it out to artists."

"Green, peaceful, and so close." Chloe peered through the sheer curtain at the lights of the Seattle skyline and tried to visualize an expanse of green, rolling pasture, "It sounds perfect, Marty."

"Easy for you to say. I'm the one who's gotta scramble and make plans. I don't even know how this cottage deal works. How many days ahead of schedule are you?"

"Fifteen and I've got three Sunday panels." Chloe walked back toward the bed.

"Okay. I'll try to get in touch with Kellerman about the rental after I call your publicist in the morning and set things in motion. And of course, I'll have to think of a tactful way to explain things to the syndicate."

"So aptly named." Chloe stared at her photograph on the cover of *Sublime*.

"Well, I'm glad to see you haven't lost your sense of humor." Marty chuckled. "Get back to your birthday party."

Chloe turned the offending magazine facedown on the night stand. "How can I thank you, Marty?"

"Save your thanks. You haven't seen this cottage yet and you don't seem to be familiar with Eli Kellerman."

"Is there something you're not telling me?"

"Maybe." Marty cleared his throat and paused. "I've heard Kellerman's a recluse who doesn't allow people to get too close. He's been described as one step down from mysterious mountain man and two steps over from snob. I've also heard about this loose-knit artists' colony in the area."

"An artists' colony? Good Lord, Marty—won't they recognize me?"

"Not a chance. This is artist as in *arty*, babe. They wouldn't know commercial. But, if you want me to look around for something else . . ."

"Didn't you say Eli Kellerman was commercial?"

"Yeah, but he hides it in his neck of the woods. Leave everything to me, Chloe. You'll be safe."

Chapter 2

PRESS RELEASE FROM PROFILES IN PEN AND INK
PUBLICIST FOR CHLOE WILDE
MANHATTAN

FOR IMMEDIATE RELEASE:

Martin Blashfield, famed business manager for, most notably, Chloe Wilde, internationally known creator of "The Wilde Kingdom," announced today that his client will take a sabbatical. Ms. Wilde will be "in seclusion with friends" in an undisclosed location during her leave of absence, which is expected to last "a minimum of three months."

Chloe Wilde has been featured in cover stories in NEWSWEEK, TIME, PEOPLE MAGAZINE, and ROLLING STONE during the past year. Her syndicated cartoon runs in 725 newspapers daily. "The Wilde Kingdom" line of T-shirts, coffee mugs, calendars, posters, and greeting cards also features the zany antics of the strip's animal and human regulars.

The self-taught cartoonist was working as a hot dog vendor when her work was discovered by the editor of a weekly Oregon newspaper. After moving to Seattle, Ms. Wilde, then twenty-five years old, gained national attention when her work was syndicated.

Known for her eccentric wardrobe and extravagant lifestyle, Ms. Wilde resides in a downtown Seattle condominium overlooking Elliot Bay. During her sabbatical, she "intends to relax from her hectic schedule" and "will be considering adding new characters" to those who frequent the panels of "The Wilde Kingdom," Mr. Blashfield said.

Eli dug his hands deep into the pockets of his faded jeans as he took inventory of the linen closet. He'd never had a woman stay in the guest cottage before. The occasion called for a few changes. His gaze journeyed from the conventional white sheets upward to the vibrant shades and patterns he preferred, and further to the uppermost shelf where the "frou-frou" bedding was stored, wrapped in tissue—and whispers from his past.

Living alone as he did, he never had use for the fragile ensembles of lace trim, eyelet ruffles, and floral embroidery, or the myriad of romantic satin throw pillows. The linens remained concealed in tissue—reminders of his failed relationship with Vanessa.

Eli leaned against the doorjamb and smiled to himself as he swept a shock of blond hair away from his face. The sight of his ex-wife's hearts and flowers had no impact on him. Time had not only given him the ability to distance himself, it had given him the resolve not to make the same mistake twice.

Vanessa had believed fully in the media-generated "brooding woodsman" mystique used—and abused—by his publicist to promote his fall tours and New York showings. The reality of life in the shadow of the Olympic mountains of western Washington didn't match her romanticized expectations, and her presence did little to change Eli's basic nature.

At times, Eli had blamed himself for being too blind to see that Vanessa had been attracted to the idea of taking him on as a cause of sorts and reforming him into a city-loving socialite. Never again would he give his heart to someone who saw his brooding reclusive nature as a challenge. In the future, he wanted to be sure women knew the difference between his public and private personas.

"Eli!"

He turned in time to see his younger brother sweep around the landing and bolt up the stairs in a blur of denim jacket and plaid shirt.

"Gabe, don't you ever knock anymore?"

"Brothers don't need to knock. I was a little surprised you weren't in the workshop." Gabe flashed an apologetic smile as he rested an elbow on the polished bannister and loosened his tie. "Why the sudden interest in the linen closet? I thought you had a special order to get out—some kind of heavy deadline."

"I do. But I'm expecting a guest."

"When?" Gabe's smile faded as he straightened.

"Today."

"Are we talking guest as in the kind of person who stays in the house, or guest as in someone who rents the cottage?"

"Guest as in *very important person*, as in *cottage*, as in *woman*. Here—do me a favor and take these." Eli lifted the tissue-wrapped bedding from the top shelf and hefted it over to Gabe's outstretched arms.

Eli grabbed the remainder of the lavender floral-and-lace pattern, and started down the stairs ahead of his brother.

It wasn't until they were at the front door that Gabe spoke again. "Eli, I think there might be a slight problem with the guest cottage."

"Impossible. I had it cleaned right after the artist from New York left." Eli glanced up at the clear sky before he headed toward the small building separated from the big house by a stream and a grove of alders. "I'd know if there was a problem."

"You get so involved in your work, you don't notice things, Eli. Like the fact that I've been stopping by twice a day for almost a week and you've never—"

"What? Your work at the newspaper isn't keeping you busy enough? This is quite a commute for you, Gabe."

"I don't think we should go into the cottage until I've had a chance to explain something."

"Explain then, and quickly." Eli paused on the wooden footbridge and glanced over his shoulder at Gabe. "My guest is due late this afternoon."

"Remember the editorial I wrote a few weeks ago about the tragedy of exotic pets? The animals and wildlife people bring out to the peninsula and release into the wild because they've grown tired of them?"

"I vaguely remember skimming that one." Eli had the uneasy feeling that he was about to get involved in another of his brother's unending crusades. "So what happened?"

"A few readers took what I said to heart and, well, to make this short, I'm the temporary holding pen for a boa constrictor and an ocelot. I'm looking for homes but in the meantime this couple brought five fertilized duck eggs and left after mumbling some story about finding the eggs in the bushes. I suspect they were bought commercially because they gave me an incubator, brooder, candler, and some elementary pamphlets on the subject. They probably got tired of the fuss."

"What does that have to do with my guest cottage, Gabe?"

"You know how small my house is, and I live in town and all. I couldn't keep these eggs at home because of the ocelot and the boa constrictor."

"Get to the point." Eli turned and started for the cottage. "I've got to make a bed and air out the rooms."

"The point is—they're in the guest house! I'm incubating the eggs in the bedroom and I've got the brooder set up."

"That's just great." Eli wiped his boots on the mat outside the front door.

"This is important. Who knows? These birds might be a very rare breed." Gabe kicked the toe of his boot against the step. "I'm not sure what type of egg we're dealing with here."

"I don't care if you're breeding dinosaur eggs— your goose is cooked if you interfere with my guest." Eli shouldered the door open and stepped inside.

"Maybe your guest will be willing to turn the eggs twice a day and spray them with warm water." Gabe's words came out in a rush as Eli stalked into the bedroom.

An elaborate forced-air incubator took up the surface space atop the dresser. Eli dropped the bedding into a chair and took a deep breath as he looked at the brooder, candler, and the cover of a pamphlet entitled *Raising Your Duck*.

Grabbing hold of a bottom sheet, he snapped it open. Gabe crossed to the opposite side of the mattress and captured the loose end. Despite the tension that hung between them, the brothers began working in tandem to make up the four-poster bed.

"Just when is the blessed event—or should I make that plural—when do you expect these eggs to hatch?" Eli waited until his temper cooled to confront his younger brother. "We're talking about a guest suffering from exhaustion. She won't be interested in watching your ducklings hatch at one in the morning, dear brother. I might share your passion for an occasional cause but I won't let you impose on my guest. The eggs have to go."

"They'll hatch in less than a week. I'm sorry but I can't risk moving them. Their condition is too precarious at this stage." Gabe was insistent.

Eli half listened as his brother blurted out a few facts about the life cycle of ducks.

"Gabe," he interrupted, "my guest is used to living a pampered existence in some penthouse overlooking Seattle. It was suggested I introduce her *gradually* to country living. Some introduction. Ducks in the bedroom. Chloe Wilde's going to think we're a couple of—"

"Chloe Wilde? *The* Chloe Wilde?" Gabe stopped stuffing a pillow into a frilly sham. "Here?"

"Her business manager called from New York to make the arrangements. He says she's a well-known artist and we're supposed to keep a lid on this. When you go into town, be evasive if anyone asks about a guest in the Kellerman cottage. She wants rest and privacy. Total privacy."

"But Eli—"

"Duck eggs!" Eli glanced over at the dresser top. "You owe me for this—"

"Eli, it's going to be impossible to keep Chloe Wilde a secret." Gabe tossed a few satin throw pillows against the shams and leaned against the post at the end of the bed. "She's a world-famous cartoonist. Her face is everywhere! Not to mention her body. She dresses in these outrageous outfits and—"

"World-famous?"

"For goodness' sake, Eli, she's practically considered something of a national treasure. Rumor has it she makes six figures a year—maybe even seven—from her drawings. You've never seen 'The Wilde Kingdom' cartoon strip?"

"Sorry, but if I recall correctly, I outgrew the funny papers about the time I reached puberty and discovered the opposite sex." Eli walked into the kitchen and threw open the windows, then moved to the sink. He turned on the faucets until the rusty water ran clear.

Gabe stood in the doorway. "You may take a sudden interest in those funny papers after you meet your guest."

Eli ignored the comment. He was too busy with his work to consider getting emotionally involved with a long-term guest. He usually limited rental of the cottage to sculptors and painters from New York. It was a way of keeping in touch with the East Coast art scene between annual showings.

If Martin Blashfield hadn't been so insistent . . .

"Stop frowning. You're still worried about the eggs, aren't you?" Gabe smiled and stuffed his hands in his pockets. "She'll love 'em. Trust me, Eli. The woman draws animals for a living. Besides, have you ever known anyone who could resist cuddling a downy little duck? It'll be a great way to introduce her to life in the country. What could be more basic than an egg?"

Eli chuckled as he stepped out onto the porch. Leaning forward, he rested his palms on the railing and gave his brother a sidelong glance. They could have been twins in outward appearance, but they were opposites, from their wardrobes to their lifestyles to their careers. *Careers.* He realized with a start that he'd just given his brother a sizable news scoop. In addition to writing mystery novels, Gabe edited the *Olympic City News*. Eli felt a sudden surge of protective feelings toward the guest he had yet to meet. Blashfield said his client needed rest and relaxation. Those words were not synonymous with Gabe "Who-What-Why-When-and-Where" Kellerman.

"Gabe," Eli ventured, "you do realize that everything I've told you about Chloe Wilde and her visit is top secret, don't you?"

"I've been standing here plotting ways I could leak the news—"

"Not unless you want a slow leak in your windpipe or one of your major veins."

"Hmmm. Okay, consider the thought abandoned."

"There's something else. It might be a good idea if you stay away from my place for a few weeks. The poor woman is going to have a hard enough time getting acquainted with country living."

Two hours later, Eli sat in his window-lined study, scrutinizing the three odd-sized books the courier had dropped off soon after Gabe's departure. The cryptic note from Martin Blashfield included a quotation from

Tolstoy. "All art has this characteristic—it unites people."

Eli opened the third in the series of *The Wilde Kingdom* books and took a sip of coffee. He set the cup down with a distracted motion. Inhaling deeply, he rocked back in his chair and leafed through the pages. There appeared to be a series of consistent characters in the panels. Human and nonhuman. Chloe Wilde put words into the mouths, beaks, and snouts of every species.

Eli sat upright. The drawings intrigued him. There were simpering lions, frogs with teeth and hair, and cows standing upright . . . and looking downright silly. For this, Chloe Wilde had become a national treasure?

Though his fine-art sensitivities were strained by the drawing style of *The Wilde Kingdom* books, there was something very likable about these characters. He could understand their universal appeal.

On the other hand, Martin Blashfield knew he was a purist. He stood and walked to the windows. How could Chloe Wilde's business manager have suggested they live in close proximity for three months?

As he sat down on the edge of his massive oak desk, Eli's hand moved up instinctively to straighten the silver dragon until it rested heavy and cool against the exposed skin of his upper chest. His fingertips rubbed against the smooth silver for a moment as he sipped the dark, rich coffee. *Ch'i.* The dragon was one of his earliest works and had become his personal favorite. It was one of his few attempts at sculpting an animal. Soon after, he'd begun experimenting with more abstract and sophisticated forms, and later, he'd discovered the nature motif that had brought him acclaim.

Ch'i was his worry bead—with talons. Eli contemplated the change Chloe's visit might have on his productivity and on him. He wouldn't allow anyone or anything to interfere with the creative process.

He'd gained widespread recognition as a silversmith, a designer and sculptor of jewelry who captured the flora of the Pacific Northwest with a realism that had become his trademark. His career was progressing with an unsettling speed that required more attention to business matters and increased productivity. He didn't have time to waste on a spoiled celebrity guest accustomed to the limelight.

Damn. Eli stared down at the cover of one of the books. He'd smiled but he hadn't laughed out loud. Had her untrained hand prevented him from enjoying her humor? Was he that much of a snob? Was he beginning to believe the much-publicized Kellerman mystique? *The earthy sculptor who created fine art.*

The silence of his mountain valley retreat was disrupted by a spontaneous and communal thunder of barking and yelping.

"What the—?" Eli rose to his feet. The armada of assorted stray dogs he'd taken in had been conditioned to ignore Gabe's truck and the usual delivery people. It could mean only one thing. He moved to the front door with lightning speed and out onto the porch.

A sleek black limousine, covered with road dust,

sat in the circle at the end of the long winding driveway. Eli's first thought was that a funeral procession had taken a wrong turn.

The uniformed chauffeur had flattened himself atop the roof of the vehicle, his face bearing a stricken expression as a tenacious terrier held him prisoner. The man kept gesturing wildly at the oak tree with his hat.

The huge oak to the right of the drive was circled by a cavalry of yipping canines.

With two leaps from the top step, Eli's feet touched gravel and he began running in the direction of the tree. Had his guest been treed? His mind rejected the thought. He was vaguely aware of the crunch of his boots on the gravel.

The moment he shouted orders to the dogs, the howling stopped. The silence that followed was immediate, profound, and overwhelming. The animals remained near the base of the huge oak, sitting on command like small statues of assorted sizes, but anxiously looking upward. Eli moved past the dogs, slowing his pace and reaching out toward the trunk to stop his momentum.

Stepping back, he glanced up into the foliage. A slender, dark-haired woman sat on one of the lower branches, hugging the tree trunk with one arm while she grasped an upper limb awkwardly with her free hand. A deep ragged cut traversed her delicate wrist.

As his eyes adjusted to the shadows of the tree's interior, Eli could make out the stranger's voluminous red skirt and bright yellow sweater. The legs that dangled beneath the hem of her skirt were encased in dark-colored tights that ended in purple high-top tennis shoes.

But the bright colors and outrageous mode of dress were forgotten as Eli focused on her face. So this was Chloe Wilde. The National Treasure. She was younger than he had expected and rather beautiful by his standards. He wasn't prepared for this. Not prepared at all.

His gaze locked with hers. The encounter with the dogs was over, yet there was an angst in her dark expressive eyes that struck a compassionate chord in Eli.

He took a deep breath, then let it out slowly. Stepping forward, he rested one palm against the oak, cleared his throat, and called up to her. "You're okay. Stay where you are. I'll climb up and help you down."

As he began searching for a handhold, he wondered how this city woman had managed to scramble up the tree so quickly. As if in search of an answer, he glanced back up at her dark oval face.

"My name is Eli," he said softly.

Chapter 3

HAZY SUNSHINE STREAMED through the lower branches of the oak tree, illuminating the man's firm features and creating a glowing aura around his flaxen hair. His pale shirt hung open, revealing a radiant object on his smooth golden chest, an object that caught and held the light with an eerie intensity.

When he reached up to grasp one of the tree limbs, there was a startling series of flickers as bright beams glinted off a ring on his finger. He was practically luminous, this Eli.

Chloe opened her mouth to protest his plan of rescue, but the man's jaw was set with determination. The sight of him moving upward make her ease her grip on the trunk of the tree.

As she relaxed, Chloe admitted to herself that she felt surprisingly secure up in the lush green cocoon.

After leaving the smoke-glassed limousine minutes earlier, the impact of the wide open sky and the expanse of fields and distant forest had overwhelmed her—almost as much as the pack of dogs that had charged toward her and the chauffeur. Perhaps she'd been too sheltered, spending almost every waking hour in front of a drawing table in her studio overlooking Puget Sound.

Marty Blashfield had promised Chloe green surroundings, peace, and solitude during her stay on the Olympic Peninsula. He neglected to mention the welcome wagon of attack animals. Though he could be forgiven for that oversight, how could she pardon his failure to warn her about the initial impact of seeing Eli Kellerman? Chloe had the uneasy feeling that relaxation would be elusive with this man in her vicinity.

The man in question was getting closer, his shoulder touching the edge of her high-top shoe. He lurched upward in one final thrust and suddenly his face was level with hers, only a few feet away.

A strong breeze rustled through the branches, blowing wavy strands of blond hair back from his tanned sculpted features. His eyes were as blue and unsettling as the open sky that had startled her moments earlier.

"I'd planned to give you a more hospitable welcome," he said in a warm, gentle tone as he shifted his body and raised one arm up to grasp a high branch. The action caused his oatmeal-hued shirt to open wider, exposing a broad, muscular chest. Chloe's eyes were drawn to the silver dragon that rose and fell with the rhythm of his breathing.

"I didn't mean to arrive with so much fanfare," she apologized. "It was Marty, my business manager. He hired the limousine and chauffeur last night. The dogs—"

"The dogs are normally well-behaved, Chlo—" Eli hesitated. "May I call you Chloe?"

A treetop was hardly the place for formalities. "You're probably tempted to call me an idiot after the way I panicked." She shook her head.

There was a flicker of amusement in his expression. Before she could assess his emotions, his eyes narrowed. "Let me see your wrist." He took her hand in his and frowned as he turned it over. "I hope this isn't a dog bite."

"No, I'm sure it happened during my Olympic tree climb," Chloe said, trying to make light of the injury.

"Hmm, it's a bit deep." Eli took a handkerchief out of his shirt pocket and tied it around her wrist. "I'll give you a proper bandage later, but I'm afraid I don't keep gold medals for tree climbing in the medicine cabinet. You deserve one, you know. This is quite a remarkable feat for a city person."

"I must give equal credit to the dogs, adrenaline, and good sneakers," she replied. "Unfortunately, I can't get down. I think I need to take you up on that offer to help me."

"I'm delighted." Eli acknowledged her remark with a smile, then moved to the limb just beneath her. "It's probably best if you climb on my back, and hold tight with your legs," he instructed. "That way you can avoid pulling on your right wrist. I take it that's the hand you draw with."

"It is, although there was a tabloid feature that claimed I have a pet baboon who draws the strip."

Eli laughed as he turned and edged into position. Chloe moved her left arm cautiously around his neck, then slipped off the tree limb and wrapped her legs firmly around his waist. She was meeting Eli Kellerman for the first time. They had yet to shake hands and make formal introductions and here she was, entwining her body around his. Her breasts were pressed against the taut muscles of Eli's back, her cheek against his hair, and her fingertips rested on the warmth of his bare skin. It would be difficult to remain aloof after this encounter.

They began their descent down the trunk of the oak.

Lord, Eli thought, fully aware of every point of contact between Chloe Wilde's supple form and his body. The woman's high-top tennis shoes were turned inward, high on his thighs. When he moved, the rubber soles of Chloe's shoes caught between his jeans and the tree. To make matters worse, his passenger squeezed her legs tighter against his waist with every jolt.

Eli was constructing a mental image of the long curve of her legs when he was struck by the vision of the two of them cast in bronze in this intimate position. The fleeting image brought a smile to his lips.

Though he may look heroic, this was one moment

The Wilde Kingdom 27

in his life he'd rather not have immortalized. His body was reacting to Chloe's presence with a will of its own and his inner thoughts were less than valiant.

"Where are the dogs?" Chloe asked when they reached the bottom limb. She tried to mask the panic she felt at the memory of bared teeth, fur, and frenzied canine bodies.

"Don't worry. They're under my control."

Chloe found it surprisingly easy to trust this man. For her, trust was a gut reaction, like choosing one taxi over another on a busy Seattle street. Most of the time, she chose to walk.

She released her hold on Eli and balanced precariously on the bottom limb. Turning, he steadied her until she mustered the courage to jump to the ground. He landed beside her just as Chloe eyed the docile canines sitting in a haphazard pattern around the tree, only yards away. Stepping back, she brushed small pieces of bark from the front of her skirt.

Eli's gaze was drawn downward by the brisk movement of her hand. He studied the details of the garish red skirt with amusement. An embroidered snake was standing upright and studying dance instructions in human footprints for the rumba. The footprints continued upward to Chloe's bright yellow sweater, where they rumbaed over one breast and continued down her sleeve.

The dance pattern led Eli's attention to the delicate oval of Chloe's face.

"I'm sorry if I caused you any extra trouble," she murmured. A muscle twitched along her jaw.

"We'll have to tie a string around your finger to remind you to stay a little more grounded," Eli answered as he buttoned his shirt. There was a hint of teasing in his tone. "You'd prefer something in a bright color, I assume?"

Chloe wondered if it had been a mistake to wear the kaleidoscopic outfit. The man looked so rugged, so natural in his chambray shirt, faded jeans, and worn boots. He seemed at one with his surroundings.

But this was his element, not hers. She felt at home in the city with her closets filled with colorful, avant-garde fashion. She'd grown to love the clothing suggested by the image consultants. Wild and imaginative, it reflected her sense of humor, and something else. Perhaps the problem of identity was part of her artistic block. The clothing, the poses, the magazine covers resonated with a sexuality that felt foreign to her. Confronting and dissecting her manufactured facade was an important part of her sabbatical. Where did that image end and the real Chloe begin?

Some part of her wished she could relive the past fifteen minutes. She'd enter the Kellerman property with grace and dignity, wearing white from head to toe and drawing the sunlight to herself. Such an entrance, though, would have cheated her out of the opportunity to meet Eki Kellerman under a canopy of sunlight and green leaves.

The sudden rumble of tires on gravel made Chloe turn her head in time to catch a wave and smile from the chauffeur as he drove past them. She whirled around. Her luggage and food supplies were piled neatly to the side of the drive. Her eyes followed a sweeping expanse of grass to a large white farmhouse set against a backdrop of tall evergreens.

"You live here alone?" she asked after a long silence.

"Uh-huh. My workshop and studio are behind the house." Eli was standing beside her luggage. "The guest cottage where you'll be staying is across the stream through the grove of alders." He pointed westward before bending to pick up two of her suitcases. "Watch that cut. Let me get these things put away, and then I'll clean and bandage your wrist."

"Don't worry. I won't strain anything," Chloe assured him, tucking a bag of groceries in the crook of one arm and picking up parcels with her left hand. They'd have to make a few trips for the cooler and other suitcases.

Chloe followed Eli over the wooden footbridge and through the trees. The quaint cottage sat in a clearing. Beyond, there was a vast meadow, a carpet of emerald green dotted with wildflowers. It was enchanting. "Do you have relatives or neighbors close by?" she asked.

"My younger brother, Gabe, lives in Olympic City. It's about half an hour west of here. As far as neighbors"—Eli pointed to a distant grouping of trees—"there's a group of artists living next door on the Camden farm. They have cows, horses, goats, and what have you. Don't be surprised to hear an occasional call of the wild. Sorry, no pun intended."

"You mean, real animals use this pasture?" Chloe

tried to pick up the thread of conversation, hoping her voice didn't belie her fears.

"Now and then. The land belongs to me but we have a barter system. I get eggs"—he seemed to choke on the word—"and dairy products in return for grazing. Since you draw animals for a living, Chloe, you'll probably find it fun getting to know the livestock. I imagine you like them quite a bit, eh?"

Fun? Chloe cast a pleading look at the vast sky that loomed blue and cloudless overhead. Fine. She could adjust to wide-open spaces again—in very little time. That challenge seemed simple.

And she'd have the alluring mystery of her chivalrous tree-climbing landlord to contend with. That she could handle.

But cows, horses, goats, and "what have yous?" How could Chloe tell Eli Kellerman she had a nervous cowardice toward all creatures, large and small? Toward anything, that is, that didn't romp within the enclosed frame of a comic strip.

Chloe looked up from the pages of *Raising Your Duck* to stare at the incubator atop the dresser beside her bed. She'd packed two-dozen best-sellers for her sabbatical. Glitz, romance, mystery, erotica, and espionage awaited her—and here she was, engrossed in a scintillating section on the incubation of duck eggs and wrapped up in memories of her first encounter with Eli.

He'd explained the presence of the incubator and brooder in the same deep, mesmerizing tone he'd used

The Wilde Kingdom 31

while rescuing her from the tree. In any other setting, she would have turned tail and headed back to the security of the city. But his voice, confident and calm, had held her there until she nodded her assent to turning the eggs twice daily. When he'd offered a reduced rental fee, she'd nodded to that as well.

Setting her reading material aside, Chloe wandered from the bedroom through the living room and into the kitchen. After Eli had left, she'd moved through the house several times, touching every surface like some territorial animal making a claim. It was an old habit, born of a traumatic childhood and her troubled years as a teenager. Knowing the cause didn't stop her from sliding her hand along the kitchen table again, or smoothing her palm over the back of an oak chair.

She settled in the window seat, wrapping her purple robe around her bare feet as she looked out at the darkened meadow. Her mood lightened quickly. She thought of Eli's gentle touch and wistful smile as he had cleaned and bandaged the cut on her wrist. There was something different about this man. She liked his honesty, sensual warmth, and playful sense of humor.

He'd helped her unpack the grocery sacks and the cooler, then stared with open disdain at the selection of staples on the table.

"What basic food group does this belong in?" he asked, picking up one of her frozen entrees. "Polar?"

"I don't like to spend a lot of time cooking," Chloe explained, taking the box from him. "Look." She pointed to the picture. "There's protein and there are carbohydrates, and look there. I think that's a vegetable."

"Where?"

"That bit of orange. I'm sure they've shaped carrot mash to look like a maple leaf."

"But, why?"

The man proved very good at asking "why" and, worse, he knew a lot about nutrition. Eli studied every entree with interest and amusing asides. The bags of cheese curls, potato chips, and pretzels fared no better under his scrutiny than had her frozen dinners.

Marty had arranged for a store in a nearby town to deliver Chloe's groceries to the main house once a week. She smiled at the thought of getting a weekly critique on nutrition from Eli. Okay, so maybe her diet wasn't balanced in the traditional sense. But she was healthy. She loved apples, bananas, and pears, and often wished there were more ready-to-eat fruits and vegetables.

Chloe looked out the latticed windows toward the meadow. Day one of her sabbatical had been enlightening and exhausting. She blinked. Were those lights flickering in the distance part of the neighboring farm Eli had mentioned? The menagerie.

Her heart began to beat rapidly. What if a rogue stallion had escaped and was charging across the fields now and spotted her, a lone female figure in the well-lit kitchen window. Stalking closer, closer in the darkness . . .

There was a loud rap behind her.

Chloe uttered a strangled half scream, raced across

the kitchen floor, jerked open the refrigerator, and hid herself behind the door, flattening her back against the meat keeper. She gasped as her breast made contact with the cold metal of the butter compartment.

The kitchen door flew open and Eli Kellerman stood in the entry, his body poised for action.

"My God, what's wrong?" he demanded, his gaze fixed on her sandwiched body. "I heard you scream."

Chloe peered over the refrigerator door. It took her a moment to convince herself the tawny man before her was not a frenzied beast. He was Eli and he was holding an ordinary phone in his ordinary hand. "N . . . nothing."

As she backed against the refrigerator shelves, her hip struck something sharp. There was a soft whirring sound and seconds later frigid water gushed onto the back of her robe. She jumped away from the ice water dispenser.

"Are you sure you're all right?" Eli persisted.

"I suffer from an overactive imagination." Chloe said each word slowly, shivering from the cold air that blasted against her wet robe and damp skin, praying Eli would leave soon. Very, very soon. "I guess I let my imagination get away from me now and then."

His features relaxed slowly and he smiled. "Don't tell me. Carrot mash shaped into monsters? Or perhaps you thought someone had put real food in there, the kind people cook on a stove."

Chloe laughed nervously. "Actually, it was just a case of the jitters. I'm fine now." She relaxed her hold on the door.

"Good. I brought your phone over. Service should start first thing tomorrow. I'll just go ahead and plug it into the jack in here." Eli walked into the living room. She heard furniture being moved and the solid click of the phone jack. He reappeared in the doorway just as she stepped away from the refrigerator.

"I'm sorry. I didn't mean to barge in but I was at the door and heard the scream and I didn't think about formalities. You might want to turn the dead bolt at night." He demonstrated the locking technique but his gaze darted to her breasts. "I don't know how to tell you this, Chloe"—he cleared his throat forcefully—"but there's something on the front of your robe."

Chloe felt an uncomfortable warmth rise from the base of her throat as she glanced down. The blush spread to the roots of her hair. It was obvious that using the refrigerator door as a shield had been a mistake. Whipped butter smeared the tip of one breast.

"Thank you," she muttered. Grabbing a dish towel, she held the meager rectangle against the front of her body, fully aware of the water soaked fabric that clung to her back and buttocks.

She raised her head. To her surprise, Eli's attention was focused on the dead bolt. Slowly, his gaze shifted—but only to her face. His features reflected warmth and understanding, rather than bemusment.

"If you're still interested in the tour of my workshop and studio tomorrow"—he stepped outside onto the porch—"late afternoon would be the best time for me. I've got a deadline and have some catching-up to do." With that simple unadorned statement, he nodded politely, closed the door, and left.

Chloe stood beside the open refrigerator for a moment knowing she should feel foolish. But she didn't. She was contemplating everything he had said and done. People like Eli were a rare occurrence in her life. She didn't know how he managed it, but Eli Kellerman appeared totally unaware of her celebrity status. It had been a long time since anyone had treated her like a *normal* human being. Chloe wondered if she'd forgotten how to respond.

Eli paused on the footbridge to glance back at the lights of the guest cottage. The whining, egotistical superstar he had expected had yet to emerge. Chloe was sensitive, gracious, self-mocking, and a bit unusual. Able to climb trees in a single bound, or at most three or four. A boutique owner's dream customer. He sensed she was something of an original, a true individual, a visionary.

He smiled at the thought of Chloe wedged in the chilly space between the refrigerator and its door, frightened by her own creative power. She had a vulnerability that shone through the colorful attire and quick wit, and it touched him. Perhaps it was connected to the pain he'd seen mirrored in those sleepy dark eyes.

Eli leaned over the wooden railing and stared down at the darkness beneath the bridge. There was no rhythm to the splash of water on rocks. The creek was as meandering as his thoughts.

It was funny. Since her arrival, Chloe hadn't embarrassed him by mentioning his own growing fame and prestige or his reputation as "the designer women would most like to touch." His work was realistic, earthy, masculine. The publicist insisted on using Eli's image to sell the Kellerman designs.

The experience was flattering. What man in his right mind would complain about photo sessions with attractive female models? The ads said it all. His work was an extension of his personality. It was just that the publicist tended to romanticize his image to the point of distraction.

Eli took a deep breath, inhaling the clean night air. And now, there was Chloe. It was wonderful to meet a woman who wasn't caught up in media hype, a woman who seemed at ease with him—and herself.

Chapter 4

"So *this* is where you create your masterpieces. I hope the offer of a tour is still open."

At the sound of Chloe's voice, Eli turned from the wax acorn he was sculpting. "Perfect timing. This is a good stopping point for me."

While his visitor stood near the main entrance, slowly scanning the contents of the display case, he followed suit with his own visual inspection. She was wearing a silk jumpsuit, the color of a tropical lagoon, belted at the waist with a lavender sash. With her dark coloring and the healthy glow of her skin, she looked like a picture of paradise.

Eli stood up and leaned against his workbench. "How are things in the incubator this afternoon?"

"Quiet. Too quiet. I've turned the eggs once and listened for pipping." As Chloe moved to the center of the room, he heard the whisper-soft murmur of silk. "Did you know they actually have a recipe for *canard à l'orange* in the back of that pamphlet? You and your brother aren't going to slaughter these ducks, are you?"

"After writing an editorial in defense of exotic animals, Gabe wouldn't dare ruffle a single feather. I'm sure the ducks will live a pampered life near town or be released to the wild. Sounds like you're becoming emotionally attached to them. Your business manager said you were suffering from exhaustion. I hope you're finding this setting peaceful and soothing—"

"It's not just exhaustion, Eli," Chloe interrupted, her tone terse. "I'm sorry. I—I don't feel like discussing it right now. Would you mind if we talked about something else? I'm anxious to hear about your work . . . and about you."

An hour later, Chloe still felt overwhelmed by the complexity of the lost wax method Eli used to create his jewelry. Even though he'd explained carefully, the important points of the process remained sketchy in her mind. She'd been distracted by the smells, textures, colors, and the array of tools in his workshop.

"—you carve the figure in wax—"

She was able to follow with her full attention in the beginning when Eli sat down at his design table and showed her the wax acorn he was carving. But her concentration had wavered considerably when she rubbed her fingertips over the worn spots in the wooden surface where Eli must have rested his elbow a thousand times.

"—surround the wax with a cristobalite investment—"

The workshop was filled with hand-carved furniture and surfaces. The high stools, chairs, and work benches were lovingly carved from rich, polished woods. There was an indication of sensual warmth wherever the eye rested.

"—eliminate the wax in the kiln—"

As Eli led her from the design area to the sink, kiln, silversmithing table, and polishing bench, he indicated the equipment, the work benches, and neatly organized tools with care and pride.

"—pour the silver into the mold to cast it—"

He loved his work, she realized, as he picked up a pair of tongs and demonstrated the intricacies of working with the kiln. Each design was an expression, a part of him, shaped painstakingly by his long graceful fingers.

"—get rid of the investment—"

Even though he was slowly explaining the tools and equipment, the step-by-step processes, Chloe found herself immersed in the man behind the lesson. The more he disclosed, the more mysterious he became in her eyes. Why was a person of such talent hiding out in the woods of western Washington? Why wasn't Eli Kellerman a household name? He encouraged her to ask questions about his craft, but she realized that the only riddles she wanted answered, concerned him.

"—and polish the finished work."

She watched now as Eli picked up one of the several necklaces in the top row of the display case. He laid it on a velvet pad. Chloe touched the smooth expanse of the sculpted leaf. Drops of dew seemed to glisten on the silver surface.

"Beautiful." She complimented Eli with the single word, hoping it would convey the high regard she held for his work.

"Let me," he offered, taking the satin strands from her fingertips. "This is a series that can be layered or worn one by one. I often design multiples," he explained. "Here. Please, turn around." He fastened the ties so the largest leaf lay low on her chest, followed by another placed higher up. A far smaller leaf completed the grouping.

Stepping in front of her, Eli snapped the leaves together, creating a cascading effect. His hand hesitated on the smallest leaf, tracing the fine silver veins with a forward movement. His fingertips slipped to the tiny stem and encountered her skin. Chloe grew steadily aware of the light pressure and the warmth of his touch.

Taking his hand away, he moved back. "This is the end of the workshop tour. My studio is up here."

Glancing up from her inspection of the necklace, Chloe saw Eli motion toward an open doorway. Even the sleek wooden steps leading up to the study were handcrafted with beautiful precision. A skylight and bank of windows bathed the room in deflected sunshine and warmth. The grove of alders offered an ethereal wall of lush green, calming to the eyes and spirit. Paintings and sculpture blended in with the tasteful elegance of the simple decor.

"What do you use this room for?"

"Thinking. Solitude. Some design work. There's a hot tub on the deck. Sometimes I soak and meditate."

It seemed an intensely personal revelation, made more revealing by the silence that followed his comment. Chloe felt mesmerized. This room had the same masculine ambiance as the workshop. Was it because of Eli's presence—or her intensified awareness of him?

She found it difficult not to deluge him with questions about his personal life and the source of his inspiration. She'd never attended classes or shared experiences with other artists. Who could better understand her creative block than someone who might have struggled through one himself?

When Eli concluded the tour of his studio, he turned to face Chloe. She was standing in a shower of diffused sunshine from the skylight overhead. He could see she was one of those women capable of transforming clothing and jewelry into something uniquely her own. Against the tropical turquoise of her jumpsuit, his cascade of silver leaves shimmered around her neck.

He looked into her soulful eyes. Once again, he sensed her vulnerability. Something was troubling her. Yet moments earlier, he'd felt awed by her power to convey strength in the defiant tilt of her chin and her erect carriage. It was her eyes that betrayed that illusion of strength.

At the moment, he felt a need to be honest with her about other matters.

Reaching out, Eli touched her arm lightly. "Why don't we relax." He led her to one of the twin love seats facing each other in front of the small fireplace. He sat down opposite her, leaned back against the cushions, and took a deep breath.

"You'll soon discover I like to be up front about things," he explained. He didn't care to tell Chloe that his experience with Vanessa had taught him one lesson applicable to both genders. *Honesty first.*

Eli looked into her anxious features. "I know this might sound odd, but I want to confess that I don't really know anything about you. I haven't followed your daily, or weekly comic strip, and I hadn't read your books until Martin Blashfield sent me copies yesterday shortly before you arrived. I'm a little embarrassed."

She stared at him, her mouth half-parted.

Eli cursed his timing. *Damn.* He was probably offending the hell out of her and he had so much more to say.

"Don't get me wrong. I'm honored to have you renting the cottage, and I'm more than willing to keep your identity a secret, but I wouldn't feel comfortable pretending to be your number-one fan. For the next three months, you'll be away from the public and the people who act as your support network—"

"I think I understand," Chloe said in a subdued voice. "You're afraid that I'm a spoiled prima donna, accustomed to praise and adulation, and that I came here expecting a daily dose of that from you. Am I right?"

"Prima donna?" Eli felt uneasy. Hadn't that expression come to his mind yesterday? Was there any polite way to express his feelings? "Well, I assumed you'd expect me to know more about you. At this moment, I know that you're a successful cartoonist with a unique sense of humor and an intense imagination and that you happen to dislike my dogs."

"That's quite a summation."

"I'm trying to say that I'd like to know you better, Chloe. It might help if I had a better understanding of how you work, how you feel about your career, and something about your personal life. I'm not trying to invade your privacy. It's just so awkward. You'll be here three months. I want you to enjoy your stay."

"I feel the same way, Eli." Chloe was hesitant. "I find it just as embarrassing to admit I've never seen your work before or even heard your name. Marty wasn't much help. All *he* said was that you were a sculptor who designed fine-art jewelry."

They stared at one another intently during the ensuing silence.

Eli combed his hair back with his hands and, placing his palms together as if to pray, steepled his fingers. "Well, we could both sit here acting insulted that we know nothing about each other," he said slowly, "or we can see the *advantage* to our meeting under these circumstances, Chloe."

Her eyes widened but he continued without waiting for her response.

"We aren't handicapped by any preconceived impressions generated by any publicity or the media."

"True." She sat forward, a slow smile curving the edges of her mouth.

"I'm probably one of the few people in this country who can form an unbiased opinion of you. For the next three months, you can let your hair down and be yourself. You don't have to live up to expectations and neither do I."

Good God! A person who didn't associate her with zany magazine covers! Chloe pondered. How long had it been since she'd signed a check or used a charge card without causing a flurry of excitement? Sometimes it was easier to let people believe what they read.

But Eli expected her to be "herself" during her stay. The same old doubts surfaced. What if she felt he didn't like the real Chloe? Would she be tempted to change colors to please him?

As a child and teenager, she was forced to play the chameleon. New cities and homes, new schools and friends, a succession of relatives and foster homes. Changing to blend in with others had been a form of self-preservation. Conform, behave, or move on.

She was an adult now, but those instincts persevered. How much of the public image had she begun to believe? What was real? Who and what was Chloe Wilde?

Eli was offering her the gift of honesty, and a special friendship. She was hesitant, frozen on his love seat like a dolt.

"It's just something for both of us to think about, isn't it?" Eli broke the silence. He was tempted to drive to the nearest library and find every article ever written about her. Last night her vulnerability touched him. This afternoon, he'd been stirred by evidence of her inner strength. The woman was growing more intriguing by the minute.

"When I read your books, I found your whimsy wonderful." Eli's hand came up to his chest to touch *Ch'i*, his one effort at being capricious. He realized with a start that he envied Chloe's ability to let go. He'd spent fifteen years perfecting his craft and, somewhere along the way, he'd lost his ability to be playful, to follow his impulses. "Your humor is refreshing," Eli added.

"Knowing something about your fine-art background, I'm surprised to hear you say that." Chloe felt the weight of the three silver leaves pushing down on her chest. She'd always been self-conscious about her lack of formal training. She'd never taken a single class in art and she was sitting across from a master of technique who considered her whimsical and refreshing. "You probably think my drawings are crude, am I right?"

"Unpolished, perhaps. I'd always told myself I'd try to be more tolerant of other art forms, other artists. I'm afraid I've turned into a bit of a snob over the years."

"And *I'm* supposed to teach you tolerance? Is that your plan?" She hated the way her voice trembled and broke. She stared ahead at the silver dragon on his chest, focusing on the creature's talons while she waited to get a grasp of her emotions. "I'm sorry," she added quickly. "You said you wanted to know how I work, how I feel about my work?"

"I thought maybe after you've settled into the cottage, you could show me how you sketch out one of your panels, give me a tour of your creative domain. I noticed your art supplies when you were unpacking."

"I'll uh—" She cleared her throat forcefully. "I'll give it some thought."

"You're upset that I consider your drawings unpolished." Eli's frank, easy manner unnerved her. "It doesn't matter what I think. The important thing is that you get your message across, and it's obvious you do that rather well. I do have a question—about the cow."

"Bar-B-Cue?" Saying the name aloud only served to remind Chloe of her artistic block. She hadn't lifted a pencil for two weeks, not since her thirtieth birthday. She missed her characters, especially Bar-B-Cue. "Excuse me," Chloe said quickly. Overwhelmed by a desire to escape, she stood up and walked down the steps to the workshop. "I think I need to be alone, Mr. Kellerman. Thank you for the tour." She attempted to untie the satin strands but soon had them knotted together.

"Allow me, please." Eli lifted the bulk of her hair with his hand. The fingers of his other hand touched the strands of the necklace. "Do me two favors. Let me untie this and let me apologize, Chloe. I've said something to offend you, haven't I?"

He was standing behind her, his words forming a soft warm wind against her neck. "I thought we were developing a nice rapport. I didn't mean to destroy that in any way. I'm sorry, Chloe." His tone was expectant.

"I'm s-sorry as well," she stammered. His hand had moved to her shoulder. The pressure increased slightly when she apologized, then he moved his fingers away to untangle the three sets of cords. His fingers were disturbingly warm and textured compared to the cool smooth satin.

"There," he said with a sigh. "I've got the knots out of these." Eli settled the necklace on the velvet pad atop the display case. "I couldn't help noticing the tension in your shoulders. You're welcome to use the hot tub. Soaking a bit might help you relax those muscles. They're probably strained by all those long hours at the drawing board. It always works for me."

How could she bring herself to tell Eli the truth? Chloe moved closer to the door, her hand searching wildly for the doorknob that would give her freedom from his questioning gaze. "You've got it backwards. The tension is from all those hours I haven't been able to sit down and face a blank piece of paper."

Eli moved toward her. "You mean—"

"I'm blocked. I've reached an impasse with my pencil. If you want a tour, all you're going to see is a woman in crisis! I'm taking this damned sabbatical because I burned out! At the age of thirty!"

"I'm sorry. I didn't know. Mr. Blashfield mentioned exhaustion but—"

"Marty Blashfield is the only other person who knows the truth about my sabbatical, Eli. I'll have to trust you not to mention this to anyone."

"It's a given. You can trust me."

She'd felt just that yesterday when they met as strangers in an airy treetop. Eli Kellerman was worthy of her trust. But she wanted him to know about her sensitivity.

"The last thing I needed to hear was the doubtful tone you used when you asked about Bar-B-Cue."

He felt awkward. "I never said I didn't *like*"—he had to search for the correct pronoun—"*her*." Cupping Chloe's cheek in his palm, Eli looked into her dark eyes. What could he say about a cartoon cow? "I guess I wanted to ask about her personality. She was struck by lightning—and now she possesses supercow powers?"

"Yes, but she's still easily startled," Chloe explained.

"By what?"

"She's afraid of other animals. Even though she has superpowers, she's shy and has to fight to overcome her desire to hide."

"Kind of Clark Kent of cows?"

"I never thought of it that way."

"And does she ever get frightened by her own imagination?" Eli stroked her cheek lightly with his fingertips. His hand moved downward until he lifted her chin with the gentle pressure of his thumb and forefinger.

Eli felt as though he were opening a Chinese puzzle box. A charred Holstein was the first clue. But where to go from here? He would have to take things slowly. Eli sensed this sudden intimacy was making both of them uncomfortable.

"Thank you." She grasped the doorknob and slowly turned it. "I really don't mean to be rude but I do feel a need to be alone right now."

"Maybe you need to be alone with the right people. I take a walk every evening after dinner. Join me tonight. I insist." The command was softened with a smile. "Nothing too strenuous. And I promise not to ask too many questions."

She stood with one foot on either side of the threshold, unable to decide. One part of her felt the tug of desperation, that everpresent need to escape. The other half, the half that held her heart, felt the pull of attraction for this enigmatic sculptor.

"I do need to keep up my exercise during the next three months," she said matter-of-factly. "And a walk is a way of being alone while you're with someone."

"If that's a yes, come up to the big house at seven. You might want to bring a jacket or sweater, Chloe—and your willingness to be yourself when you're around me."

"You make it sound mandatory."

"It is."

Chapter 5

"I BOUGHT THE farmhouse and property about five years ago." Eli stuffed his sweat shirt pocket with dog biscuits while he patiently answered another of Chloe's questions. "My priority was getting the workshop and studio set up. When time allows, I'll add some touches to make the big house feel more like a home."

"It already feels like a home. Just look at this big old kitchen. I love the smell of firewood and the faint whiff of spices—and all the windows!" Eli was fascinated with the way Chloe gestured so freely as she praised his antiquated farmhouse kitchen.

"I think we're ready. Here, just put some of these in your pockets." He dropped a few of the biscuits into the pocket of her oversized sweater. "This way," he pointed. "I always go out the back." He shouldered the screen door open, then held it as Chloe slipped past to stand on the porch. "As you can see, this is the favorite part of the day for my—"

"Dogs!" She pronounced the word with more breath than voice and recoiled back against his body as six assorted canines came to life at the bottom of the stairs.

"Stay!" The dogs obeyed his command immediately. "I can make them stay home if you'd rather not have them walk with us."

"Do they walk ahead or behind you?"

"A little of both—and then some. They have a lot of energy but they'll be too busy chasing each other to bother us. I promise you, the Kellerman hounds will behave."

With Eli close behind her, Chloe squared her shoulders and moved down the steps cautiously. "I guess this is one sure way to get acquainted."

"And it's one sure way for me to get a chance to ask *you* questions."

"No fair. I'm on sabbatical," she announced with a little shrug. "I believe that entitles me to diplomatic immunity from questions."

"Then I'll keep it simple." Eli slowed his pace to match hers. They were walking on the narrow dirt path that led to the south meadow and on to a wooded area by the creek. "When did you start drawing 'The Wilde Kingdom'?"

"When I was barely eight." Chloe appeared startled by her own quick response.

"Inspiration started young for you."

"I'm not sure if you could call it that. I-I was living with my great-aunt Meade in the Oregon countryside. She had cows. Holsteins. Something happened—something in the back pasture—and suddenly I was terrified of all animals except these black and white creatures. That's when Bar-B-Cue was born."

"You created her to protect you?"

"Exactly." Chloe bit her lip. "A mild-mannered Holstein until she moseys into a phone booth and zap! I spent a lot of hours alone as a child until I started drawing her. Even now, she's still my funny little supercow."

"And the other characters? Where did they come from?"

"Bar-B-Cue needed someone to rescue so I built a community greatly in need of occasional aid." She tilted her head and smiled softly. "When I was eight, Bar-B-Cue was an island of stability in my life. I could trust her to be there for me."

"Is trust an issue with you?"

She kicked a rock in the dirt path, then paused. Bending over, she picked up the rock and studied it intently. "My mother abandoned me when I was seven, Eli. I can't think of any softer way to say it. It's one part of my history that's never gotten into print. I haven't lied exactly. I've just sort of focused on other parts of my childhood to create a smokescreen. Did you have one of those terrific carefree childhoods?"

"Pretty much." Eli watched as she tossed the rock

up and down in her palm. "So you grew up on your aunt Meade's farm?"

"No. I stayed with her for six months before I moved on. It wasn't easy bears."

"Easy bears?"

"Just one of my favorite expressions, Eli. I'll translate—life wasn't easy. I was passed from relative to relative, and later, there were foster homes. New schools, new neighborhoods, and friends, new rules. What I needed was continuity. Every kid should have a portable supercow like Bar-B-Cue."

"Maybe it was your sense of humor that helped you survive those years."

"Survive?" She looked up at him with widened eyes, her mouth half-parted. "Survivors don't always escape unharmed, Eli. I'm proud of my career and all the success but . . ."

Her expression grew wistful, then contemplative. Eli felt a need to reach out and touch, to comfort her, but he recalled Chloe's request for time alone, her desire for privacy.

He'd taken many a walk alone and knew there were times when a friendly touch would have been welcomed. Eli slipped his hand in hers. Chloe's only reaction was the gentle pressure of her fingers curled through his.

For several minutes, they walked on through the meadow in silence, the dogs romping playfully ahead of them. Spring wildflowers completed the idyllic tapestry of lush green grass, a dusky blue sky, and the faint glow of moonrise.

It was Chomp, a sad-eyed rascal of questionable ancestry, who approached Chloe first, wagging his broken tail with abandon.

"Over here, boy. Here, Chomp," Eli commanded. The dog ignored his master, choosing instead to follow at some distance beside Chloe.

"What breed is he?" she asked with a laugh.

"Well, all the dogs are strays, so we can't be sure. But my brother thinks Chomp gets his height and coloring from a Dalmatian, his pugnacious look from a bulldog, and his brains from a dinosaur of some kind."

"So he's not overly intelligent?"

"You might say his light shines a little dimmer than most, but his heart's in the right place. And his stomach appears to be a bottomless pit. Try tempting him with one of those dog biscuits."

"Those are dog biscuits in my pockets?"

"What'd you think I'd given you?"

"Whole wheat snacks of some kind." Chloe let go of Eli's hand and took a green triangle out of the pocket of her sweater. She inspected it warily. "Good thing you warned me, Mr. Kellerman."

Eyeing the dog treat, Chomp moved closer, whining pitifully. When Chloe kept her distance and failed to hand over her biscuit, he circled her and began limping dramatically.

"Eli, this is one smart dog. I kind of like him. Broken tail and all. What made you assume he was *dim*?"

"That's my brother's conclusion. Chomp wouldn't learn tricks like the other dogs."

"Then he's *super*intelligent. Why jump through any stupid hoops? I was the same way as a kid. I listened to a decidedly different drum. In fact, I think the whole orchestra in my head was a bit offbeat."

Eli held out a biscuit but Chomp looked away, continuing to eye the green triangle in Chloe's hand. With exaggerated dramatics, the dog began dragging his hind legs behind his body, stopping occasionally to cough.

"Chloe—you better give him the biscuit. You don't want to see the finale."

"What more could he possibly do?" she asked with a frown.

"A death scene. The choreography alone is staggering. Believe me," Eli said drolly. "We've reached the trees. Chomp could hurt himself. He doesn't just roll over and play dead."

"Of course not. He's one of a kind. Like me." Hesitantly, Chloe extended her hand toward the dog, offering him the treat. Like a consummate actor, Chomp dragged his body toward her, his sad-eyed expression brightening somewhat as he neared his goal. "Good boy. Good—uh, Eli, I have one question. Did you name this dog Chomp because he bites people or because of his appetite?"

"Don't get the jitters now . . . he's almost there."

"Teeth or appetite?"

"Appetite."

The dog struggled forward, took the biscuit from her hand with a minimum of teeth, and ate it slowly as he studied Chloe's face. The green triangle was followed by an orange bone, a brown square, and a yellow circle.

"All gone, boy." With a trembling hand, Chloe reached out to pat the dog's head. She skimmed the tip of one ear with her fingertips. On the second try, she let her palm rest on the black-and-white spotted hair atop his head. "You're so soft, Chomp. You with the sad, sad eyes. I wonder why your people abandoned you."

Her last comment touched Eli to the core. He'd been wondering the same thing about Chloe Wilde.

Slender beams of fading sunlight filtered through the trees, highlighting the creek's meandering path and glistening on the wet rocks. Chloe took a deep breath and released it slowly. Purposely relaxing made her feel all the more conscious of the bands of tension coiled in her shoulders and across her chest.

She watched Eli move effortlessly across the large stones in the creek as he played fetch with five of the six dogs. She'd climbed up to this vantage point soon after they arrived. Walking with the dogs was one thing, standing among them as they ran helter skelter was quite another.

Though she was limber and kept her body fit with aerobic workouts, she envied Eli's ease, the loose trusting way he positioned his feet on slippery surfaces. She tried to imagine her own slender body darting from rock to rock but the picture was made up of hesitant steps and faltering handholds.

Could she pull a stick from a dog's mouth and toss it into the lengthening shadows? Where and when did people learn to let go? When did they learn to trust the dog wouldn't bare his teeth, the stick would fall without injuring, the water in the creek would only be ankle deep?

Chomp sat by her side, seemingly disgusted with the infantile behavior of his canine colleagues. She marveled at the soft texture of his coat and the intelligence she saw reflected in his mournful eyes. Her newfound friend nestled his body against her as if to force her hand to stroke the top of his head and down his back.

"Do you call this your secret place?" she cupped her hands to ask Eli. He'd grown quieter as they walked through the wooded area to the creek. Playing with the dogs had lifted his mood to one of playful exuberance.

"It used to be a secret place," Eli mused. "I came down here when I wanted to be alone, but the dogs insisted on following. If they could, they'd drag the UPS man down here and coerce him into tossing sticks for them." He began making his way toward her. "The rascals would have no qualms about opening a concession stand. It's dog heaven. The place belongs to them now."

"So where do you go when you really want to get away from it all?"

"The mountains. That's one of the reasons I wanted

to live on the Olympic Peninsula. I do a little climbing with friends. I know it's a paradox, but sometimes I go to Seattle for a day of anonymous living. There's nothing like being in a crowd to make you feel alone, Chloe. You look a little surprised."

"I am. Surprised, that is. Marty said people consider you reclusive, but you're saying you go mountain climbing with friends or get lost in a crowd to feel *alone*?"

"Reclusive doesn't mean antisocial. I'm just a bit of a lone wolf. Hell, part of that mystique is manufactured to sell my work."

Eli looked over his shoulder and whistled to the dogs. "Time to pack it up!" he shouted. Turning, he focused his gaze on her. "I hate to disturb this peaceful scene but we should start back before the sun gets any lower in that sky. Here—" He offered his hand. "Those rocks look dry, but you might slip on the moss."

She took Eli's hand without hesitation, appreciating his steadying force as she climbed down to the flatter rocks near the bank of the creek. When both of her feet were secure on the grassy knoll, Eli stepped back and studied her intently, his fingers still entwined through hers.

"I'd love to photograph you in this light. It's almost surreal . . ." His voice grew thicker. "The drama of the sunstreaked clouds gathering behind you and the silhouette of the trees. And your face, Chloe. Your incredible face."

She tensed, waiting for the standard comments

about her bedroom eyes and full mouth. She felt a keen sense of disappointment. Eli hadn't seemed like the others. He'd talked about their getting to know one another without preconceived opinions. That thought had rolled through her mind several times during their walk, and it had pleased her. Why did he have to mention photographing her?

Eli smiled and looked beyond her to the creek. "You know, sometimes an artist wants to capture a moment that is more emotion than it is content or lighting or composition. I think that's what I want to remember. Your expression and the way you looked back at Chomp."

"Chomp?" Chloe became aware of the dog's nose touching her open palm. She didn't recall glancing back at Chomp when she reached the bank. She remembered accepting Eli's hand and feeling his strength, enjoying the warmth of his hand and feeling secure.

"There are some emotions we don't really have words for," Chloe said, taking a step to close the gap between them. "Like what I'm feeling now."

"And what's that?" He smoothed a tendril of dark wavy hair back from her face.

"Safe. What a strange word. It doesn't say enough of what I'm feeling."

"Don't be so sure, Chloe. I believe it says more than enough. Come on," he urged. "The meadow is beautiful in twilight."

Hand in hand, they retraced their steps back to the farmhouse in the fading light. She listened as Eli described the changes that came over the landscape in summertime. Their conversation softened to a comfortable silence.

She felt Chomp's nose touch the back of her hand from time to time. "I think I made a new friend today," she commented with a laugh.

"Make that *two* new friends," Eli said softly.

By the time they reached the footbridge leading to her cottage, Eli's arm was resting on her shoulder.

"You've been here two days. Is the cottage comfortable enough?"

"It's perfect. If I have anything to complain about, it'd be the quiet, perhaps. The quiet still keeps me awake."

"Keeps you awake?"

"I'm used to urban noise. Car traffic, buses, planes, trains, sirens, and the foghorns and other sounds from the waterfront. I don't know. The noise makes me feel so alive."

"And now? You feel *safe*, right?"

"Yes, safe. I remember saying that."

"You know"—Eli stepped closer—"I've had a lot of city dwellers rent the cottage. The isolation and quiet take time to get used to. It's the same for everyone."

"Did any of your former tenants suffer from a creative block?"

"Not exactly. A lot of them came here to recharge. Maybe that's a bit of the same thing. But no one's ever stayed for more than a month. I would think your three months might seem like an eternity if you get anxious about the block and don't make any progress in working through it." His fingers brushed her neck and then moved to her cheek. "Chloe?" Her name was a gentle entreaty.

She placed her hands on his shoulders, then slid them slowly down to his well-muscled chest. The edge of her thumb touched the outline of a dragon talon beneath the rough fabric of his shirt.

"Your dragon makes me think of magic. If only it could be that simple—breaking through this wall. Of course, there's no guarantee about what I'll find on the other side."

"Or *who*. Is there anyone special in your life?" His fingertips brushed hair back from her temple.

"Special? No. At this time in my life, my career is everything. It always has been." The warmth of his hand on her cheek was distracting her. "I . . . I never thought it'd be fair to subject anyone to my erratic schedule or my moods."

"Not fair?" He stroked his thumb back and forth over her lower lip. "I'll probably get to see my fair share of your moods during the next three months. I'm beginning to look forward to every one of them." The movement of his thumb stilled on the fullness of her mouth. He brought the textured pad up to trace her cheekbone. "I'm a little concerned, to be honest, about how you'll react to *my* moods."

"Are you temperamental?" She heard a warm rasp in her own voice and knew it echoed the desires his touch was stirring.

"Terribly."

"I thought you said recluses weren't antisocial?"

"As a group, we're generally misunderstood."

"You're making me laugh intentionally, Eli. Why don't you just tell me to lighten up?" She smiled at his expression of mock surprise. "I don't know why—but I feel so good tonight."

He pulled her closer, his hand a firm pressure that moved down to the base of her spine and rested there. "I'm glad to hear you're feeling good." His mouth hovered over hers, heating her lips with his breath. "You'll feel even better . . . when I kiss you."

His mouth silenced her attempt to protest. Tenderly, he molded his lips to hers. She surprised herself, responding with hunger, as if this were the uncertain magic she'd been seeking. She closed her eyes, and as she did so, she became aware of all of him, the solid wall of Eli's chest, sinewy forearms, his gentling touch.

It was all too much, too soon.

The need to escape, the pull of attraction. Chloe felt as she had earlier in the day when she stood with one foot on either side of Eli's threshold.

It was so early in her sabbatical. Eli could become a trusted friend, an ally in her time of turmoil. Would it be a mistake to rush into anything more intimate than that—to be swayed by her physical desire?

She broke from the kiss and lay her cheek against his chest. She wasn't able to make a choice as she had on the threshold. She was beyond that.

"Eli, I'm not sure about this," she whispered into the hollow of his neck. "I liked feeling safe."

"You are safe. You don't need to run from me, Chloe. I think we can learn a lot—from each other."

"I'd like that." Her voice had regained its strength. "But I'm not sure about the affection . . . or the intimacy. Not yet. It's not you. This has nothing to do with who you are. It's me.

"Eli, you've been wonderful today." She relaxed her arms until her hands rested on his chest, then leaned back and looked up into his eyes. "I'm going to accept a few of those invitations you made—to use your hot tub and your study now and then. I like the skylights and the view of the alders and . . . it's peaceful. I'd use them for reading and thinking and relaxing. I'm not even ready to think about when I'll begin drawing again."

"You have a lot on your mind, Chloe. Your whole future, for one thing. I don't think you needed the extra pressure I put on you tonight. Let me give you a nice platonic hug." He embraced her gently. "I'm sorry if I upset you." Eli held her a moment before stepping away and resting against the railing on the opposite side of the footbridge.

Chomp moved to Chloe's side, resting his head against her denim-clad thigh.

"I see that I'm not the only male seeking your company tonight. He's such a smoothie." Eli leaned over to pet the dog. "I should get back to the workshop. Why don't you let me walk you to the door of the cottage, Chloe."

"No, that's all right." His platonic hug had felt so inviting, she wasn't sure if she could open the door without asking for an encore. "The security light's on," she added in a cheerful tone. "And I have Chomp."

Chapter 6

ELI GLANCED UP at the workshop clock just as he finished polishing the last silver acorn in the new design. Two A.M. He was tempted to lock up and retire to the big house to catch up on his sleep, but figured he had enough energy left to assemble the oak leaves and acorns on their cords of satin and silver.

It'd be one more piece completed for the upcoming show in Seattle. Eli unfolded the packet of velvet-wrapped oak leaves he'd finished earlier in the week. Gathering a handful of satin strands, he began weaving them through the silver clasps he'd designed for this particular multiple. He felt the heavy heartbeat of anticipation as he added the leaves and acorns, and the design became a reality he could hold in his hand.

Only one other moment compared to this. The moment he draped one of his necklaces around a woman's throat. Large groupings such as this sold well, especially when the sculptor was present to demonstrate.

Suddenly Eli flashed on the image of Chloe, the afternoon two days ago when he'd placed the multiple layering of leaves around her neck and smoothed them down with his fingertips.

He recalled every detail; her heart-shaped face, the graceful way she held her long slender neck as he adjusted the necklace. And her eyes. Sultry but seemingly filled with warring emotions. Defiant yet fearful.

She was like a kaleidoscope, changing with every turn. Tumbling with emotion but landing on her feet. Easily read one moment, cloaked the next. Mysterious. Haunting. Lovable. Why had she hidden in the guest cottage for two days?

Eli completed the grouping before turning off the workshop light, locking up, and walking down the well-worn path to the farmhouse. The back-porch light illuminated the screen door. Attached to the door was a large piece of paper, its edges fluttering in the late-night wind. Eli took the wooden steps two at a time and tore the paper from the wire mesh.

Eli,
I didn't want to bother you while you were working but the ducklings have been emitting noises since yesterday and now they seem to be slowly breaking through their shells.
I've read the book and it's a lot more compli-

*cated than I realized. I'm not asking for your
help as much as I'm simply afraid something will
go wrong and we might lose a duckling.*

*Chloe
11 P.M.*

In the halo of the dim porch light, he read and reread the hastily written note. How could he have forgotten about his brother's precious duck eggs? Knowing about Chloe's deepseated fear of animals only heightened Eli's irritation with himself.

Hard as it was to admit, she'd hurt him the other night when she moved out of his embrace and stammered a lame excuse that registered strongly on his machismo meter. Had the memory of that moment caused him to withdraw, to ignore his duties as host and landlord? As newfound friend?

His hours were erratic during deadlines. It was easy to become obsessed with seeing a project through to completion. Except for a brief nap, he'd been awake since yesterday morning. The day before yesterday to be exact.

As for the care and feeding of eggs, he knew as much about duck babies as the Three Stooges. What kind of intelligent help could he offer Chloe in his sleep-deprived condition?

He stood on the back porch, his hand moving up to touch the dragon *Ch'i*, waiting for the voice of reason, the inner knowing he'd trusted since childhood. and immediately he knew that just being there for Chloe would be enough.

Eli shrugged off the exhaustion and made his way to the cottage, calling for Chomp every fourth or fifth stride.

He was crossing the foot bridge and still no dog had appeared. Eli suspected the black-and-white stray had somehow charmed his way into the guest house *and* the heart of their guest. *Lucky dog,* Eli thought as he knocked on Chloe's door.

"I saw your note—"

"Oh Eli, I'm so glad you came!" Chloe greeted him enthusiastically. "Four of the ducks have hatched but the fifth is having trouble. It's all so complicated— you know, all this hatching stuff. Temperatures and humidity and brooding—"

"I'm supposed to be good at brooding," he interjected.

"Eli, I'm serious." Her eyes widened as she pronounced the word *serious*. She closed the door and leaned back against it. "The first four are doing great according to the handbook your brother left, but the fifth duckling has barely made his way around the— Please come into the bedroom! Quick!"

"Chomp?" Eli choked out the name.

Chomp was sprawled at the foot of the four-poster bed, exuding a regal air. The dog, who had always refused to enter Eli's house, was immaculate, his coat neatly groomed. He cocked his head as if to acknowledge the presence of his owner.

Eli nodded back before he caught himself. He turned his attention to the crisis at hand.

From her position in front of the five-drawer

dresser, Chloe watched the incubator with an anxious expression. "Over on the right—see? The duckling has circled all the way around the blunt end of the egg but it can't seem to pop the lid off. The poor thing—can you hear those muffled chirps?"

Eli was more startled by the appearance of the four ducklings inside the incubator. They appeared wet and weak and defenseless. "You watched the four eggs hatch without calling me?"

"I wrote a note at eleven and stuck it to your door when I figured the big event was near. Disappointed?"

"It's not that. I was thinking of the inconvenience. Gabe and I never intended to have you lose a night's sleep over this. I'm really sorry, Chloe."

"Please, don't be." She flashed him a forgiving smile. "It was a wonderful experience, especially for someone who's always been afraid of birds and animals and reptiles." She chirped back at the tiny ducklings in the incubator, who raised their heads and stretched their necks in response.

"What does the book say about helping birds out of their shell?" Eli picked up *Raising Your Duck* and flipped through the pages.

"You'll find the section on page one eighty-three. I don't agree with them."

Eli quickly skimmed the section, then closed the book. Some experts advised against giving too much assistance to live ducklings imprisoned in their shells after the hatch. The struggle, according to the book, was nature's fitness test to weed out the weak.

"How much help is too much?" he wondered aloud.

"I'm not sure." She stepped to one side, frowned, then looked down at the bedroom rug. "That book also says hatching activity stops during the night, but look at these four little night owls in the incubator. I don't know. Maybe I'm being impatient about egg number five but the others hatched much faster. This bird could simply be exhausted. I think I'd feel a lot better if I just tried to help a little."

"You could try breaking away a bit of shell," Eli suggested. Chloe opened the incubator and slipped her hand inside. Touching a finger to the cap of the egg, she gave a gentle nudge, then quickly withdrew. The splintered shell fell away, revealing a tiny occupant.

"I wonder what its mother would do—if she were here. *Come on, live, little b-baby.*" There was a break in Chloe's voice that tore at Eli. "Is it moving?"

Standing beside her, he felt a protective urge envelop him. How could he take her away from the pain he heard echoed in her voice? His feelings had nothing to do with her physical capability to deal with the situation. In his eyes, life had dealt her too many blows. It was her courage in the face of emotional fragility that had touched him again and again since her arrival.

How much help was too much?

He placed his hand at the small of her back. "Let's give it a little time," he suggested in a whisper. "You already said there was a possibility this duckling could simply be exhausted."

Brief seconds later, the small bird kicked its legs and escaped the remainder of the egg. When Chloe gasped, the duckling lifted its head and emitted a soft greeting.

After Chloe returned the call several time, she leaned against Eli. "Well, this is certainly something I don't encounter every day back in the city." She tried to stifle a yawn and failed.

"You're tired, Chloe, Can we transfer them to the brooder now?"

"Not until they're fluffed out and get a little stronger, which can take several hours. I have to watch the temperature and humidity in the incubator for a while before I prepare the brooder."

"This sounds like a full-time job. Why don't you let me help? These eggs were my brother's responsibility—"

"You're as tired as I am. You've been hiding out in your workshop for two days, Eli." Stepping back, she sat on the edge of the bed.

"Me hiding? I've been working. I thought *you* were avoiding me because I rushed things a bit the other night."

"I'm not the recluse," she teased. "I confront issues."

"Issues such as?"

"Such as naming the ducks." She jumped back up and walked up to the incubator. "The first four have a head start on Moses."

"Moses?"

"Seems like a good name for the last duck, doesn't it?"

"I like it. And the others?"

"We could be commercial and go for the glamour names like Donald and Daffy and Daisy."

"Baby Huey wasn't one of my personal favorites as a kid but I think he was a duck." He sat down on the edge of the bed. Chomp scooted forward and Eli rubbed the dog's ears.

"Eli, you read comic books?"

"Of course." It'd been a mistake to sit on the bed, he realized. The comfort of the mattress made his aching muscles yearn for sleep.

"What made you stop reading comic books?"

"Sports, girls, and everything else that interests a thirteen-year-old. I couldn't afford comic books *and* the pleasures of adolescence. Back to duck names, Chloe."

"How about unisex names like Waddles, Ping, and Pong?"

Letting his feet rest on the floor, Eli leaned back on the bed. He might as well get comfortable. Didn't Chloe say the ducks wouldn't be dry for hours? "Nice choices, but then . . . you're something of an expert."

The bed seemed to absorb his ability to think and speak. He looked up at Chloe's slender frame. She didn't seem to be aware of his floating state. She stood in front of the dresser, totally absorbed with the contents of the incubator.

He had sudden urges to get totally absorbed in the

long dark hair that tumbled down her back. *So beautiful*, he thought.

"What makes me an expert?" Chloe asked with a laugh.

"You dream up names for cartoon animals and . . ." He closed his eyes for a moment.

"These ducks are different, Eli." Her voice sounded far away. "They're just a little more real."

Chloe awoke feeling strangely disoriented, knowing something was different but unable to pinpoint what change had occurred as she slept. Small chirping noises coming from the side of the bed brought the facts back into focus for her. She peered down at the brooder. She'd set the metal cage on top of an old chest so it wouldn't be directly on the floor. Five pairs of anxious eyes stared back at her.

The eggs had hatched. The ducklings were healthy. Sometime in late morning she had awoken in a semiconscious state and moved the downy little ducks from the incubator to the brooder. Upon returning to bed, she had discovered a fully clothed Eli Kellerman occupying the opposite side, and a gently snoring Chomp snuggled closely to the footboard. She'd thought it wise to let the dog out, leaving only one dilemma. Eli.

She'd fallen asleep debating whether to disturb him. Judging from the sunlit scene outside her window, hours had passed.

Still drowsy, Chloe turned her head. Eli was still there by her side, sleeping soundly. She found this man far more interesting than the most terminally cute baby duck.

His shirt buttons had come undone in the restless throes of sleep, revealing the expanse of his tawny gold chest to her gaze. Words came to her mind. Words like *strength* and *power* and *warmth*.

It was Eli's quiet strength and the warmth of his words that drew her to him. It was the element of trust, an uncanny sensing she felt the moment they met, that kept her close enough and open enough to learn the man.

Lying next to him like this, she was able to study him intently. His even features, firm mouth, and high cheekbones had no doubt been photographed repeatedly to advertise his designs. How had he appeared to any woman scanning through the slick pages of a magazine? Hadn't Marty mentioned mountain men? Rugged. Self-reliant. Determined.

How could there be a conflict in personas? Eli was all of those things. Had his chest been bare? Had those magnetic blue eyes worked their magic on film?

Chloe rested her head on the pillow and sighed. Even in repose, there was a defiant set to Eli's chin. The shadow of his beard only magnified his rugged masculinity. Her feelings for the man were just beginning to sprout roots. If she lay here ruminating for another ten minutes, she'd talk herself into forever afters. It could be easy.

"Eli," she whispered, reaching out to gently touch his arm.

His eyes opened slowly and appeared immediately clear, all knowing, unstartled.

"Good morning, and *good night*!" He covered his face with his hands for a moment. "I didn't meant to stay—it must be noon. What's that noise? Wh-what happened to the ducklings? Have you moved them yet?"

"See for yourself." Chloe sat up on her edge of the bed and pointed toward the chest. "They're settled in their brooder, eating me out of cornmeal and water, and demanding my attention."

Eli stood up and began buttoning his shirt as he walked around the end of the bed. He squatted down in front of the brooder. "They look happy, but don't they need something to swim in?"

"Not necessarily. The book says to wait two weeks."

"Do you always go by the book, Chloe?"

"I've never raised ducks before. The author has. Why?"

"I guess I'm just anxious to see them swim."

"Great. Two weeks from today, we'll have a swimming party." Chloe quacked at the ducklings, alternating between high notes and a rather low note.

"And which one is Moses?" Eli asked.

"The one with the deeper-than-normal quack." Chloe knelt down beside Eli. "Hear that? Moses is a bit of a baritone. Ping, Pong, Waddles, and Daffy are just plain noisemakers."

"They're more than that. Chloe, I think these ducks

may have imprinted on you. See—they're not paying any attention to me at all."

"You mean—" Chloe sat down on the rug. "They think *I'm* their mother?"

"Congratulations." Eli sat back and rested against the dresser.

"But I don't look anything like them," she protested. "I have dark hair and dark eyes and—they're yellow and gray with black racing stripes."

"They could be Mallards," he observed wryly. "You're incredible, Chloe. When you arrived five days ago, you were seemingly afraid of all animals. So far, you've befriended Chomp and hatched five ducklings. Maybe *fear* is too strong a word for you to use."

"What do you mean?"

"Thinking you're afraid might intensify your fear. For example, do you think maybe you're *afraid* to draw?"

"That does seem to be part of it."

"Tell me about it. When did it all start, Chloe? Or should I say, when did it stop?"

Chloe paused for only a moment. The memory was still so vivid. The events that had occurred since then paled to the pain of the first realization.

"It started the morning of my thirtieth birthday. I had a vague idea shaping in my head, so I sat down at my drawing table and discovered I couldn't get the idea from my brain to the paper. I felt devastated. My cartoons are everything to me."

"Turning thirty is an important milestone for most people. Sort of a time for reflection."

"And goal setting. I discovered something this year. I've achieved all my career goals—in a period of less than five years."

"I guess your challenge is to set new goals."

"It's not just that, Eli." She pulled her legs up and hugged her knees with her arms. "Look at my life. I'm too comfortable. I don't have any concerns about finances or housing or work or *anything* really."

"Is being comfortable the same thing as being happy, in your eyes, Chloe? Are you happy?"

She didn't answer. She released her legs and took one of the ducklings out of the brooder and held it in her cupped hands.

"I don't have to worry about material things either, but I'm still searching for . . ."—Eli paused—" for something. A kind of inner tranquility, perhaps."

"Not me." She smoothed her palm over the duck's downy back. "I know this will sound strange, Eli, but please refrain from laughing. I think I need misery to feed my muse."

"Misery?"

"Hardship, struggle, emotional highs and lows, some good old-fashioned strife. I thought I asked you not to laugh."

"I'm just smiling broadly. I like you, Chloe Wilde. I like you a lot. And I think you've come to the right place for your sabbatical. Some people, experts like Gabe and my former wife, claim I'm something of a pro when it comes to creating misery."

"You seem almost proud of that."

"I believe they're wrong." His voice gentled. "I'm hoping, Chloe, that I might be able to give you some insights into your creative block and learn something about myself in the process. A few nights ago you said I made you feel safe. But that was before I kissed you and upset you. I care about you, Chloe. Affection is an expression of that caring."

"I feel the same way, Eli. There's something special happening between us. It's just that I don't want complications. I like you so much as a friend."

"Friends can stay friends. And friends can make understanding lovers, Chloe, but I'm not trying to rush you. We have to do our weekly shopping tomorrow. How about a picnic the day after? If you like, we can take the ducklings on their first outing in the meadow next to the cottage. It'll be sunny and warm—"

"No swimming yet, right?"

"Right. Don't worry, Chloe. I won't let you wade too deep."

Chapter 7

"WHAT'S ON YOUR shopping list anyway?" Eli glanced over Chloe's shoulder at the small slip of paper she was holding close to her face. "Hmm, all it says is 'frozen foods.'"

"I believe you referred to my diet as consisting of the polar food group when you helped unpack my groceries the day I arrived." Chloe reached up to adjust her straw hat and to smooth a few errant waves back under the brim. She then gave her shopping cart a playful shove. "Is it really necessary for me to make this weekly trip? Marty Blashfield said the store would be happy to deliver."

"I didn't think it'd be smart to take a chance on the delivery person arriving an hour early or a few hours late and recognizing you, Chloe." He lowered his voice when speaking her name. "This way you only need to wear your disguise while you shop."

"No one will give me a second glance, right?" Chloe asked with a laugh. "I mean, why *wouldn't* anyone in the town of Two Corners notice the weekly appearance of a woman with all of her voluminous black hair shoved up under a straw hat, and wearing a white sundress and reflector sunglasses and—"

"So I'm not equipped for disguising my guests." Eli shrugged and dropped a loaf of whole wheat bread into his cart.

"—a woman who keeps her shopping list at mouth level to hide her most recognizable feature," Chloe continued, "those incredible bee-stung lips."

"Well, you know what's good for bee stings."

"Ice," she answered without a pause. "I'll be in the frozen food section."

"Whoa, a bit compulsive, aren't we?" Eli commandeered her cart, "Why don't we visit produce first. Fresh fruit and vegetables—"

"I read somewhere that compulsion will become the faddish neurosis of the nineties."

"Thank you for informing a recluse such as myself. I can begin honing my skills now." Eli relaxed his grip on her shopping cart, then removed his hand completely. "I admit I'm a bit controlling at times."

"Like when you tell other people to improve their diets?" Chloe stepped over to him and slipped her arms around his waist in a gentle embrace. "I like that in you for some reason, Eli. Your concern seems so genuine. I mean, if *I* have a more balanced diet, it doesn't really benefit *you*."

He bent down to kiss her forehead. "It does if I don't have to eat a frozen entree on tomorrow's picnic. I confess my motives are purely selfish. I'm ready for the nineties."

She took off her sunglasses and studied him for a moment. Her smile was wistful. "You know what I like for bee stings, Eli?"

"Something better than ice?"

"Much better. A friendly kiss. One or two steps up from platonic but something suitable for the bread aisle."

"Like this?" His lips brushed hers as he spoke, then returned to devour the half-parted softness of her mouth. Eli felt a heat stirring within. She was so willing, so giving of herself as she'd never been before.

"Chloe," he whispered against her cheek when they broke the kiss. He felt her body sway against him. The bodice of the white sundress drew his attention downward to the swell of her breasts. "Was that kiss suitable for the bread aisle?"

"No." She shook her head. "I think we need to step over to the aisle of spice, Mr. Kellerman."

"I can understand your reluctance to bring the ducklings, Chloe. These Cornish game hens we're eating"—Eli set a tiny drumstick on his plate—" would have traumatized them for life."

"It wasn't just a poultry problem." Chloe straightened a corner of the faded plaid blanket they'd spread out over the lush meadow grasses. "Your weather prediction of sunny and warm was too optimistic." She followed Eli's glance upward. Brisk winds moved the puffy white clouds across a blue sky. "The ducklings have to be kept at ninety degrees during the first week of life, so I figured they were better off at home in the brooder.

"Besides," she added, "I didn't want to be distracted this afternoon."

"From what? The scenery or the food?"

"From *you*, Eli." Chloe looked directly into his eyes. "Without a dog or a duck or one of your designs or sculptures or one of my cartoons in sight. Just us. Just the people we are."

"You make it sound so easy. You're a rather complicated picture even when you're alone, Chloe. Getting to know you is a bit like walking through a maze. But then you're one labyrinth I wouldn't mind getting lost in."

She smiled back at him. Then, looking down, she began to pick at the food on her plate. Eli could only guess that his comment had made her uncomfortable. When would Chloe realize how special she was? And how could he make that realization easier for her?

After yesterday's shopping trip to Two Corners, he'd invited her to join him in the hot tub water after dinner but Chloe had declined. Politely. Succinctly. Without explanation. Not that an explanation was necessary. He just couldn't understand why she didn't want to build on the wonderful web of intimacy that had developed in Two Corners.

"Are you disappointed that I'm not funnier?" she asked out of the blue. "People always seem to expect cartoonists to be uproariously funny."

"I didn't have any expectations when you arrived, Chloe, and I still don't. I like your sense of humor and I love to hear you laugh. It sort of echoes through the labyrinth."

"And you're calling *me* complicated? Look who's talking. You're pretty complex yourself. I know more about Chomp's mysterious past than I do yours."

"I've been as open as I need to be."

"Right. I know you have a brother named Gabe who writes mystery novels and works for a newspaper and protects the rights of animals. You grew up in Seattle and your parents still live there. And I know that you were married once. You said something about your brother and your wife thinking you were an expert at creating misery." Her voice softened. "I thought that was a very telling statement."

She picked up the bottle of wine and offered him another glass of Chablis. "What is your ex-wife's name, Eli, or am I out of line here?"

"No. You wouldn't ask unless you wanted to understand me a little better. Her name is Vanessa. We've been divorced for two years."

"So she lived here—in the farmhouse?"

"Just for a short time. When things started breaking down, we had an arrangement of sorts. So many weeks in Manhattan, then back to Washington State and so forth."

"Vanessa didn't like living here?"

"Hardly. The first time she walked through the house, she passed judgment on every room and proceeded to tell me how she would throw out this or that and use these colors and—well, I didn't mind the thought of renovation but she was talking about creating a house that bore no resemblance to my home. It was destruction. On her terms."

"Sounds like you were real opposites. How'd you meet her?"

"In New York at the opening of one of my shows at a trendy boutique. I swear she fell in love with the brooding-woodsman mystique used to promote my work. You know me, Chloe. There are times when I retreat inward to focus on my work, but I consider myself warm and outgoing and easy to live with. I'm opinionated about some issues, the issues that are important to me. And I think I'm sensitive when it comes to dealing with other people."

Eli paused to sip his wine. He had never found it easy to talk about his failed marriage but today his thoughts flowed smoothly. He wasn't gripped by the playback of ugly scenes. His tone was conversational rather than angry or resentful. He realized for the first time that many of his old hurts had healed.

Chloe sat across from him on the blanket, her head cocked to one side, her dark eyes reflecting her interest and concern.

"I still think Vanessa saw my reclusive nature as a

challenge. When I grew quiet—either because I was contemplative or because I was designing in my head—she was affronted. She was determined to reform me into a city-loving socialite, yet at the same time, she was enamored by the image of the strong, bullheaded man who would put her in her place occasionally.

"I'm not blameless, Chloe. I can be eccentric. I've always collected stray dogs, and I like long walks, and now and then I disappear. To do a little mountain climbing or roam the city for a few days or hang out with old friends."

Eli paused., "I won't make the same mistake again," he added.

"What mistake?"

"In the future, I want any woman who claims to love me to have a clear understanding of my public and private personas."

"And exactly what is that difference?" Chloe asked. "Are you sure a clear understanding is even possible?"

"A person would have to see the ads and the articles. Maybe observe me during one of my openings." Eli laughed. He laid down on he blanket and looked up at her. "I'm sorry. So often I forget you don't know that side of me—the side that others are usually so familiar with."

"It's the same for me, Eli. I wish there was a way we could reveal our public selves to each other—while I'm still living here."

"Maybe there is. We can each call our publicist and

ask that packets of press clippings be sent. My packet will be for you and your—folder will come to me."

"Sounds fair," Chloe agreed. "Actually, it sounds like a bit of fun."

"Yeah, it does. Are your bee-stung lips really your most recognizable feature, Chloe?"

She was sitting beside him on the blanket, looking down into his face. She rested her hand on his chest. "You'll find out," she teased. "I never knew there could be so many different ways to photograph the same body."

"Tell me, how do you want people to really see you?"

"As a professional cartoonist who's earned the right to be proud of her success." Her voice was clear and calm. "There's no other word for what I am, Eli. I'm a highly paid, hard-working *professional*." She seemed to savor the word. Then she frowned. "I know what I don't want to be. I don't want to be a fluke. Or the sex symbol of cartooning. Or a flamboyant joke."

Eli reached up and linked his hand through hers, pulling her down beside him on the blanket. His arm moved around her waist. "You said you were a pro just now and you were pretty emphatic about it. The important thing is that *you* believe it. To hell with anyone who doubts your ability."

Her body tensed beside his. "That subgroup wouldn't include you, would it, Eli?" The softly modulated tone of her voice altered. She inhaled sharply and frowned. "Soon after I arrived, you referred to my drawings as unpolished, if I remember correctly—"

"I explained it all then—"

"And you admitted you'd turned into a snob and needed to learn tolerance." She swallowed hard. "How do *you* explain the phenomenon of my success? I have to wonder if the words *professionalism* or *talent* come to mind."

"Chloe—"

"No, it's not just you, Eli." She touched his cheek. "Maybe life is like this. Being admired for your work isn't enough. People need a little extra magic if you want them to remember your name. I thought the title of my strip was enough. 'The Wilde Kingdom.' How blatant does it have to be?"

"You really love your work, don't you?" Eli drew her closer. "You get so passionate about it."

"I adore it. I have the best job in the world. If I hadn't gotten syndicated when I was twenty-five, I would have kept trying long past fifty. It's all I've ever wanted to do."

"Maybe you should use the future tense. Wipe all thoughts of the block out of your mind and visualize what you'll be doing three months from now."

"I'll be negotiating for a new contract with extended vacations guaranteed every year. You meet the nicest people on sabbaticals."

Eli was amazed. The storm clouds that had crossed her features and darkened her words minutes ago lifted as quickly as they had arrived. Chloe was resilent.

Because he worked alone himself, he understood. There were no coworkers to nudge him out from under a dark cloud or to bring him down from a celebratory high. He had to become aware of his own moods. Through studies and meditation, he'd learned about choices long ago; the choice to turn toward sunlight no matter how small the beam, no matter how dark the room. Even then, the lessons were ongoing, incomplete, fragmented. Life had dealt him few blows.

He sensed that Chloe had learned about choices as a child, learned to hide her tears and use her humor as a defense. Life had been her classroom. He admired her spirit, her tenacity, and the honesty she was willing to share with him.

He felt the fleshy contour of her breast as she snuggled against him. She was wearing a long purple sweater and a short denim skirt that left an enticing stretch of thigh open to his appreciative gaze.

Eli reached over to his half-finished plate and slipped something from the edge of the dish. "This morning when I baked the game hens, I decided I'd save the wishbones . . . for us. They're not dry yet, but we could give this one a try."

He held one half and waited for her to grip the other.

"Give me a little time," Chloe pleaded. "This will be tough. The wishbone is still so slippery! And my mind just went blank. I can't think of anything, Eli."

"How about a little misery to feed your muse?"

Chloe laughed and tugged playfully on her end of

the wishbone. "If I ask for misery, I'll probably get more than I can handle."

"Then we'll search tonight's sky until we find a star, Chloe. Don't ask for less misery. Ask for the strength to cope with the misery you asked for. How's that for convoluted?"

"All this wishing seems like a lot of effort just to deal with a creative block."

"Maybe what you really need are doses of strong emotion. Higher highs and maybe one lower low."

"Are you offering to introduce me to these stronger emotions, Mr. Kellerman? What's first on your list?"

"Joy," he said softly, pulling on the small wishbone. The bone gave a feeble snap.

Using the soft pressure of her fingertips, she angled his mouth to fit hers. Her lips stroked over, against his, in a kiss that was gentle but thoroughly arousing.

"You won, Eli," she observed. "Joy it is."

"Did you come to visit me or the ducks, huh, Chomp?" Chloe greeted her canine visitor late that evening. Chomp remained positioned on her doorstep emitting a shallow whine. "What is it, boy? Come on. Why won't you come in?"

It was then that she discovered the cardboard box on her porch. Intrigued, she picked it up and took it into the kitchen where she set the box on the table. Chomp followed eagerly beside her.

The brooder sat on the floor. She had gotten into the habit of moving the ducklings to whatever room she was going to be in. Whenever she was out of their sight for too long, their pitiful cries echoed through the small cottage making it difficult to ignore her status of "mother," imprinting or not.

At the moment, her attention was focused on the mysterious box. She opened the first flap and found a hand-scrawled note that said simply *More joy, Eli*.

Her eyes grew misty and she held the note to her chest. The picnic she'd shared with Eli had already become a memory she would hold dear, no matter what their future together held. The man was capable of taking a simple wishbone and creating a magical moment.

They'd spent an hour in each other's arms, sharing kisses and talking softly about Eli's upcoming show in Seattle and the pressure of deadlines. She sensed his restraint and for a space of a few minutes, resented it. There was a passion stirring within her unlike anything she'd ever experienced. To admit it and expose her need would be contradictory. It was she who had talked of her need to feel safe.

She no longer felt any impulse to escape at the first threat of intimacy. When his mouth captured hers and time became a long continuous silver thread coursing through her veins, she gave in to the feeling, she wanted to drown in the pools of sensation his closeness brought.

"More joy, Eli." Chloe read the note aloud a second time before slipping it into her pocket. Opening the second flap, she found a huge mound of clay. She lifted it out of the box and onto the kitchen table, conscious of her own shallow breathing. She searched for a second note and, finding none, pondered the meaning of the gift.

He was a sculptor. Not just of the jewelry designs. She'd seen some of his large work. Maybe it was natural for Eli to have plenty of clay on hand, but why would he give some to her? Chloe wondered.

She ran her fingers over the top and sides of the lump, enjoying the texture, recalling the myriad of clay animals she'd formed in grade school. The image of Bar-B-Cue came to mind. The cow had changed little over the years. Chloe hadn't been able to draw her favorite character for more than two weeks. What if . . .

She sat down at the table and stared at the mound of clay in front of her. Digging her fingers into the top of the mass, she pulled off a handful. She reacquainted herself with the feel of clay, enjoying the malleability of the medium. It felt wonderful.

She rolled out a portion of it on the oilcloth that covered the tabletop. Then she began to shape the familiar bovine body. Rising, Chloe grabbed a few toothpicks and a small knife from the counter. Quickly returning to the table, she became absorbed by the simple project.

Chomp moved to the opposite side of the table and peered through the slats of a chair.

"Have I ever told you about Bar-B-Cue, Chomp? No? Well, she was struck by lightning when she was very young—that's why she has a racing stripe down her head and back. It was a hair-raising experience for her, but she recovered."

Chloe felt a shiver of excitement as Bar-B-Cue began to evolve into a recognizable personality. Or personalities. Like Chloe, she had learned the art of being a chameleon. "You see, Chomp," she continued, "Bar-B-Cue's a party cow one minute, sensitive listener the next. This mild-mannered member of the herd can be transformed into a superpowered heroine and defender of justice within seconds.

"You're going to like her, Chomp." Chloe widened her eyes at the adoring dog across the table. "She's got black-and-white spots just like you, sort of the yin and yang of life if you know what I mean."

Chloe leaned back and studied the clay cow's facial features. Using a toothpick, she added more charm to the smile and gave the eyes a "woeful but willing" touch.

Fifteen minutes later, when she completed her creation, she was more than satisfied. She'd felt every dimension of the little cartoon cow. It was like pulling back and looking at herself, imagining the complexities but seeing in reality the simplicity of it all.

The experience resembled nothing short of a rebirth. Bar-B-Cue was born of a little girl's anguish, the anguish of abandonment. From the ashes of that lightning bolt, there rose a means of viewing life anew.

Chloe stood up and smiled at the perky cow in her palm. Why should she waste a wishbone asking for misery when optimism was her trademark?

She glanced at the clock on the kitchen wall. Eli was working double time to make up for the long leisurely picnic. As much as she wanted to see him, to thank him for the gift of clay, she hesitated to disturb him.

Instead, she sat back down at the table and, once again, she contemplated the mound of clay and the gift of joy.

Chapter 8

THE PRESS CLIPPINGS and photos and posters arrived three days later.

Nothing could have prepared Chloe for the shock.

Eli Kellerman stood in all his primitive glory against a surreal forest setting. A narrow beam of light, hazed with swirling dust motes, chanced across his forehead, igniting a golden shock of hair. Eli, his chest artfully displayed, was surrounded by a half dozen women wearing nothing more than raw-silk loincloths and concealing shadows. Female ears and throats, wrists and fingers shone with the splendor of the Kellerman designs.

Expecting a relaxing afternoon of reading, she'd heated the bedroom to a stifling temperature only a baby duck would appreciate, and donned a long cotton T-shirt. It had taken fifteen minutes to create a protective border of pillows around a portion of the bed. When all was ready, she released the ducklings from their brooder for a bit of exercise with their imprinted "mom." The exercise course consisted of climbing over her toes.

The two overnight express packages had arrived together. Chloe and Eli had agreed to spend the afternoon perusing the contents in private before meeting at eight that evening to discuss their reactions.

Since opening the large package, Chloe had lost track of time, and she'd lost almost all conscious concern for the five tiny ducks stretching their necks and clamoring for her undivided ducklike attention. She chirped every thirty seconds or so and kept her body low to the bed to assure the ducklings she was close.

But that was true only in the physical sense.

Her mind was on another level of reality, focusing on the highly erotic images of Eli that lay scattered before her.

In a rain-forest setting of ancient, moss-covered trees, the sensual textures of wood and moss and vine were highlighted with an ethereal light. Eli draped a necklace around the slender throat of a woman dressed in formal evening attire. His hands were posed in a gentle caress. Hanging from vines about him were the silver designs inspired by his close proximity to the Olympic Peninsula's Hoh Rain Forest.

Chloe touched her fingertip to the photo, tracing over the beads of water on the silver surface of a leaf.

She'd viewed only a portion of the package's contents, yet she felt even more envious of Eli's fine-art training. The man created beautiful objects to wear and to admire. These treasures were lasting. He could look at nature and preserve that moment forever.

Her comic strip was as transitory as newsprint. How many times had Bar-B-Cue's image ended up lining the bottom of a birdcage? Or rubbed noses with a fish?

What had Eli said? He studied and worked for years to perfect his craft. Her characters had evolved only slightly during the past five years, usually when she discovered minor errors made in drawing animal anatomy. Did she need to challenge herself in some way?

She was enormously successful. People loved the crude drawings and the humor and the optimism. What was the saying? *If something ain't broke, don't fix it.* How would she ever know her full potential unless she used these three months to experiment?

The smallest duck took a tumble off her foot and immediately looked up at her, crying pitifully.

"Poor little Moses tripped on my toeses and almost broke his noses," she sympathized in a singsong voice. She touched the top of his head and smoothed her finger over his down-covered back. "You'll end up being a real featherhead if you don't get some coordination. When you grow up into a beautiful Mallard, I'll come visit you on Mother's Day or you guys can fly over to Seattle and land on my balcony and visit me."

The duckling quieted and Chloe returned to her task of getting a firmer idea of Eli's public image. She looked at the photographs spread out on the bed. He was aloof in many of the poses, almost to the point of being arrogant. Self-involved? Utterly male. Vain? She continued looking through the photos, searching for the words to define how he contrasted with the Eli she knew.

Just the glimpse of Eli's wedding portrait struck her with unnerving force, an almost painful impact felt in her chest area long before she fully comprehended the nature of the photo. So this was Vanessa. Blond, petite, animated, sophisticated. Chloe skimmed a few of the clippings. Vanessa had a background in art history and owned a thriving boutique in Manhattan.

That was enough. It was all Chloe needed to know. She didn't want to feel compelled to be like or unlike Vanessa in any way. Relationships between people were not only unique, they were private and filled with mysteries outsiders weren't always meant to explore.

It was Eli Kellerman she cared about. She continued glancing through brochures and posters and clippings. The private Eli she'd come to care about refused to merge with the Greek god posing in natural settings with assorted female models displaying his designs.

Opening the package had only confused her. Eli the enigma had simply become Eli the erotic enigma. She gathered the materials together and turned her attention to her flock of Mallards. After a few minutes of play, she was struck with an idea.

Why not keep a photographic record of her sabbatical for publicity use and for her own personal archives? Nothing sexy or provocative. The photos would reflect her private self. Working with clay, playing with the ducklings, taking her daily walk in the meadows with Chomp. She'd ask Eli when they met at eight o'clock.

And perhaps Mr. Enigma would let her turn the camera on him from time to time. She wanted to preserve her memories of the private side of Eli Kellerman forever.

Nothing could have prepared Eli for the shock.

He'd opened the packet from Chloe's publicist while sitting in his window-lined study in the big house. Within five minutes, he moved to the seclusion of his bedroom on the second floor, away from any remote possibility that someone might peer into a window and see these startling images of Chloe Wilde.

Chloe clowning in exercise gear. Chloe reaching for the sky in funky red overalls emblazoned with row after row of black-and-white cows moonwalking. Chloe accepting awards in provocative evening wear. Chloe smiling and autographing her books but looking somewhat overwhelmed as a crowd in a bookstore pressed close.

She graced a few dozen magazine covers, with close-ups and full body shots. Bright colors were her signature. It was clear her publicist felt Chloe wasn't fully dressed without a smile. Granted, it wouldn't seem right to have a cartoonist frown at the camera, but Eli felt betrayed. Where was the reflective, vulnerable, and often fearful side of the woman he had grown to know?

Had the creative block affected her that greatly? Or was Chloe a chameleon of professional caliber, able to keep her private persona truly private?

Two years ago, she'd joined other celebrities posing for a fashion spread on intimate apparel. Chloe's slender but curvaceous body was shown to its best advantage in a red satin teddy and sheer robe. She was standing beside a well-known comedienne. The two women were laughing, but the candor didn't break the sensual mood of the photograph. If anything, it added an extra dimension to his understanding of Chloe. She'd been able to relax while posing half-nude with a stranger in front of Lord knows how many other strangers.

For long minutes, he couldn't sort through the emotions he was experiencing. He was angry when he thought of how her beauty and innocence might have been exploited. His protective streak rose to the surface.

Why did she have to be so damn photogenic on top of everything else? No wonder the magazine editors adored her. He couldn't blame editors. If Chloe's fans didn't respond to her zany poses, she wouldn't be asked back. And no doubt there were plenty of male fans who had been stopped in their tracks by her dark-eyed beauty staring at them from a magazine cover.

Did men make passes at autographings? Eli wondered.

She frolicked and cajoled and danced through a dozen fluffy profile pieces, each ensemble a little more daring, more outrageous than the last. Was there any color that didn't look good against her café-au-lait skin? It was as if Chloe owned rights to the rainbow . . . and according to knowledgeable sources, the pot of gold as well.

Gabe had been right. The incredible Ms. Wilde was wealthy. It was obvious she wasn't conspicuous or foolish about it either. She'd hired others to handle her affairs, leaving herself free to create her comic strip and live a rather reclusive existence.

A few articles concentrated on the evolution of "The Wilde Kingdom" strip. One displayed a picture drawn by Chloe at age nine. The essence of Bar-B-Cue the Cow—humor conquers all—was evident even at that early age.

There was no mention of her abandonment. Chloe glossed over her childhood in interviews, mentioning a Moroccan father she could not remember, and a mother who encouraged her child's artistic streak at an early age. She admitted the comics had been a solace to her during troubled times.

Eli wondered who else knew how troubled those times had been. Was he making too much of it? Why did she have to be so brave about the pain she'd endured? Was her humor some kind of shield she held up against the agonizing truth? How could he become a part of that shield to make her emotional burden lighter?

Eli looked out his bedroom window at the billowing tops of the alder grove he shared with the guest cottage. How he wished he could send her thoughts that would help lift her creative block. When he closed his eyes, he recalled that first meeting in the top of the oak tree. Her eyes had been filled with an angst that reached out to him. He'd never lost that feeling, the desire to offer an arm or a shoulder or to stand still, squelching his own desire when a silent sharing of a moment meant more.

She talked of her teenaged years as being typically awkward and painful, avoiding mention of foster homes and relatives who passed her from town to town like a hot potato. A hot potato with a heart.

Eli read on. He arranged photos in chronological sequence to study the changes success had brought in Chloe Wilde's outward appearance. Her coltish beauty at twenty-five had been softened by the use of sophisticated makeup techniques and hairstyling. But the essential Chloe, the bee-stung mouth and haunting eyes, would never change.

He was filled with envy for her ability to smile and play for the camera, for her public, to lose herself in a humorous moment.

Chloe's visit had forced him to look inward at his attitudes about art and artists, about people in general. He had become something of a snob. Eli knew it. Each time he glanced at the cartoons that accompanied the many articles about Chloe, his eye drew a critical circle around some small flaw in perspective or anatomy. He needed to flex his funny bone more often.

The final article that caught his eye was a haughty piece by a psychologist attempting to analyze the public's response to "The Wilde Kingdom." Eli smiled at Dr. Liddicott's complicated theories. Was it important to understand why Bar-B-Cue the Cow tugged at people's hearts? He was still perplexed about Bar-B-Cue's creator and alter ego.

After meeting Chloe and reading her three books, he'd quickly realized that in some strange way Bar-B-Cue represented the child that remained a child within Chloe. Bar-B-Cue the Cow was frightened of other animals despite her supercow powers. But place a cloak over her—Eli paused in his thoughts—over her prime ribs, and she was fearless.

What magical cloak did Chloe put on before posing for her public? What gave her the power to rise above her fears?

He turned his attention to the photo that accompanied the psychologist's article, a profile shot of Chloe at her drawing table. What would happen if her creative block was permanent? If her inspiration never returned? He'd turned the question over frequently while reading the articles.

He knew she'd been shaping animals with the clay he'd left on her doorstep. Perhaps that was the first step. During their picnic, he'd suggested doses of strong emotion . . . beginning with joy. What emotion would be next on the list?

Eli reached into his shirt pocket and took out a small box. Designing, sculpting, and completing Chloe's gift had eaten up valuable time in his busy schedule. If he hadn't followed his impulses, however, it would have been impossible to concentrate on work.

Opening the box, he stared for a moment at the delicate gift of gold within. Tonight, perhaps, they'd explore even deeper emotions.

Chapter 9

AT EIGHT O'CLOCK that evening Chloe found the door to Eli's workshop open. She thanked her ever-present companion, Chomp, for escorting her from the cottage, and let herself in. As she walked toward the stairs that led to the studio, she paused to glance into the glass display case filled with Eli's elegant designs.

Never had his work looked so beautiful, so unique, so very real. For the first time since the start of her sabbatical, she felt truly awed at the thought of living so close to the famous Eli Kellerman.

She walked up the stairs slowly, stopping on the top step to enjoy the spectacular scene outside the bank of windows that lined the west side of the large L-shaped room. The last scarlet rays of sunset cut like frozen shards of light through the alder grove, casting a warm glow over the outer deck and the polished wood floor of the studio.

When the packages had arrived earlier in the day, Eli had suggested they discuss the results of their experiment while soaking in the hot tub. It was a nightly ritual for him, a ritual he made reference to more frequently as the two of them had grown closer.

A glass roof offered shelter from the elements but gave the area a feeling of openness and freedom. A futon, for lounging in the sun or sleeping under the stars, Chloe guessed, was cradled by a hand-carved base that extended out from the woodwork lining the sides of the deck.

White candles were scattered throughout the area. They caught the scant light reflected from inside the studio and glowed eerily, reminding her of Eli's deeply spiritual nature.

Chloe took a deep breath. When would the lacework of panic that had invaded her body begin to fade?

The tasteful touches, the artful design, the rich look of wood—this was all part of Eli, she tried to reassure herself. The deck both reflected his artistic nature and his rugged masculinity. It was simple, romantic, direct, aesthetic, powerful—like the man.

In the gathering darkness, Chloe could see the bright red light on the control panel. The timer was on. The water was heating. There were expectations. Hadn't she agreed with him when he suggested soaking in the hot tub might be an easy way to discuss their experiment? She envisioned the erotic photo of

Eli in the rain forest setting . . . the jungle setting . . .

The distinctive pop and crackle of a fire permeated the dreamlike mood she'd slipped into. Turning, she found Eli at the far end of the studio, sitting in front of the fireplace, stoking the fire and staring into the flames.

She watched him for a moment, seeing him as she'd never seen him before, feeling uneasy as she looked for clues to his mood. Had he looked through all the material sent by her publicist? Was he feeling as disoriented as she was?

She stepped closer and felt overly sensitized to every nuance—her random thoughts, the movement of her foot, her breathing, the temperature of the room, the taste of wild strawberries that lingered in her mouth from her short after-dinner walk with Chomp.

"A fire in June?" Chloe asked. She told herself to relax. She sounded so stilted, so forced. Why hadn't she started off the conversation on a more intelligent note?

"A fire in June." Eli looked up and smiled. "It's not that unusual. I light fires year round."

It was so unlike her, but Chloe was immediately aware of the sexual implication of his remark. She would avoid talking of fire. She'd come here with a purpose, to discuss her reaction to their experiment. That was the subject at hand. Public and private personas.

So why did she want to fixate on his smile? He

seldom smiled in his photographs. Brooding woodsmen don't smile. Her only encounter with a woodsman was from reading about Red Riding Hood. The real Eli had a radiant smile and used it frequently.

"Pardon me for pointing this out, but you're staring, Chloe. Must be the fire. Sort of hypnotizes a person, doesn't it?"

"Yes."

"Did the ducklings wear you out again today?"

"I let them out of their prison and gave them a chance to exercise on the bed. Don't worry about your linens, I put a few sheets of drafting paper down first." She crossed the room slowly. Looking down, she noted the way the crimson rays of sun shone through the skirt of her pink sundress. Why was she so suddenly self-conscious?

"How did you react to our experiment?" Eli asked.

"I'm not sure. I haven't formed any concrete opinions yet." Chloe stood behind the love seat opposite him. "W-what about you? Have you looked through the pictures and articles and the whole package?"

"More than once. Why are you so nervous, Chloe? Come here, sit next to me. Take a deep breath and enjoy the fire."

She *was* nervous and couldn't understand why. With trepidation, she sat down by his side on the love seat. How could she begin to explain her feelings?

"Maybe . . . maybe it's because I feel like we're meeting for the first time all over again. Maybe it's because I know I've done a lot of foolish things just to get my name in print and I think you'll—"

"Come on, Chloe." His tone challenged her. "Those things couldn't have been any more foolish than some of the things I've forced myself through."

"I don't think I'm ready to talk about my public self or your public self." She felt even more defensive. "I'm still—I don't know. It reminds me of something that happened long ago. Something painful that I thought I'd forgotten. Just now it came to mind."

"Can you make it come to your *lips*? Don't let my teasing bother you. Can you tell me about this incident from your past?"

"I'll try." Chloe took a deep breath. "It wasn't a big incident—it's just another example, perhaps, of the way I've masked my feelings to please other people.

"I was living with my aunt and uncle and their five kids and having a tough go of it. I must have been ten or around that age. I was always so sensitive, Eli. I swear I wore my heart on both sleeves." She paused to gather strength against the unshed tears burning her throat.

"I was reading the paper and saw photos of these two kids who were up for adoption. My mother had left me three or four years earlier and I'd heard relatives talk about giving up hope that she'd return and how I might be adopted out.

"So adoption was this very real thing to me. I studied the faces of the kids in the newspaper and I wondered how they felt—sort of like their whole life depended on how they looked in one tiny picture. The boy was smiling and the girl wasn't. I figured she'd made a pretty big mistake." Chloe recalled that moment of realization as if it were yesterday. "I remember telling myself that I would smile for every picture when I found myself in similar circumstances."

"And you still smile for every picture, right?"

"That's too simplistic, but I guess so," she said with a faint laugh. "Maybe what I'm trying to say is I don't want to feel as if I'm being judged all over again."

"Then we *won't* talk about our experiment for a while, all right?" Eli put his arm around her shoulder and pulled her close. "Look at the fire. Just stare into it and let your thoughts drift. It'll help you calm down."

Chloe focused on the flickering flames, but found herself distracted by the feel of his fingers moving up and down her arm. Stroking, softly stroking. All thoughts of her troubled childhood eased. She basked in the warmth of the fire and the comfort of his arm around her.

"Growing up in Seattle, I was close to lakes, rivers, the Pacific Ocean. I found that being close to water made me peaceful and reflective," Eli explained, his free hand moving up to touch the dragon on his chest. "But for some strange reason I've always drawn strength from fire."

Chloe found his voice as mesmerizing as his touch. It was as if her sense of hearing and touch had become suddenly acute, suddenly one. When he spoke of fire, the word became a living thing that grazed the sensitive planes of her body and made her aware of her own inner heat.

"My love of fiery things drew me to my career and helped cinch my decision to buy the farmhouse," he went on. "I work with molten metals and kilns and—I have five fireplaces in the big house and this one in the studio. And then there's the hot tub."

"The hot tub?" she echoed. "What does that signify in your realm of fire?"

"The perfect combination of water and heat, peace and strength, reflection and renewal." He looked directly into her eyes. His hand moved up to touch her cheek. "Perhaps, Chloe, it would be the perfect place for the two of us to begin getting to know one another better."

"Eli?" She half choked his name.

"I'm sorry, I didn't think I was being overly direct. It's just that"—he stroked her cheek with the pad of his thumb—"the images from the photos—they're still floating around in my head. Our experiment answered a lot of my questions . . . but it created a few new questions as well. And it made me realize just how very special you are. To me."

"You don't have to explain now, Eli," she said, shaking her head. "I feel like I'm spinning. There's this collision in my mind—one image of you crashing against another and yet, they're all the same. I guess."

"Thank you." He nodded. "For taking the time to find the words. And Chloe, if you feel the least bit reluctant, let me know—"

She put a finger to his lips and smiled.

The fire created a surrealistic halo of warmth behind his blond head, a halo of diffused light that gave his startling blue eyes an aura of innocence and calm. Chloe felt the gentle pressure of his hand on the small of her back.

When he stood, she rose with him. When he offered his hand, she took it. When she stepped through the door to the deck, he followed.

The night air was surprisingly warm, but then, Chloe recalled as she looked up, the deck was protected by a glass roof and glass walls that extended some distance from the sides of the studio. The effect created a cocoon of warmth and intimacy.

"There's mineral water on the table if you'd like to pour a couple of glasses," he suggested.

"Of course." She was glad to have something to do with her hands.

Wordlessly, Eli picked up a set of matches and lit a candle. Picking up that first candle, he ignited another and then another, moving slowly around the deck seemingly without pattern until every creamy white candle glowed translucent in the gathering darkness.

Chloe was fascinated with this image of Eli. Lover of fire. Keeper of the flame. With his luminous hair and radiant eyes and sculpted features and that mystical dragon on his chest . . . She didn't have to close her eyes. The haunting images in the slick photographs were there, ever present, as clear and real as the taste of wild strawberries that lingered in her mouth.

The Wilde Kingdom

Eli was about to become her lover. That meaning was implicit in his remarks, in the lighting of the candles, in the easy silence that had replaced their meandering conversation.

The only doubts that remained in her mind had to do with her own inadequacies. She'd had only a few brief romantic liaisons in her life. Her lack of trust had always been the biggest obstacle to forming a lasting relationship.

Eli can be trusted, she reminded herself. The doubts lifted. He walked toward her, still holding the candle he'd used to ignite the gallery of light. When he paused for a moment as if to contemplate her, she felt the warmth of the flame reflected in his eyes.

"Chloe." He spoke her name so gently, the flame shuddered softly and flickered over his features. With a graceful movement, he set the candle on the edge of the hot tub.

Eli lifted his T-shirt over his head, exposing his chest to her appreciative gaze. "Come here," he whispered, pulling her into his embrace. His lips stroked lightly over hers until she swayed against him. Her mouth softened and parted, accepting the gentle exploring thrust of his tongue.

Her arms encircled his waist. She stroked the firm, well-developed muscles of his back, which tensed beneath her fingertips while their kiss deepened.

"Chloe." He croaked her name. "I feel like I've already memorized every inch of you. Remember the photo of you in the red silk teddy?" His fingers moved up the sides of her arms. "You had this attitude, as if you were totally unaware of how sexy and vibrant and beautiful you looked." Slowly he teased the straps of her sundress off her shoulders. "Laughing with your head tilted slightly back and your wonderful mouth—" he paused.

"I remember the photo," she quickly interjected, unable to resist a smile. "It's a favorite with male fans. I've been asked to autograph it often enough. I take it you liked that one, hmmm?"

"It made me have some rather wicked thoughts."

"No." She feigned surprise. "About me?"

"About what I'd like to do *with* you . . . tonight, Chloe." The bodice of the sundress slipped to her waist, revealing her firm, high breasts. He inhaled sharply.

The warm night air felt like a caress against her bare skin, but she wanted only to feel the caress of this very special man.

"Touch me, Eli. I want to feel your touch."

He cupped her breasts reverently, circling her breasts with his fingers, teasing his palms over the dusky rose peaks. He felt her nipples harden beneath his touch.

"You're so perfect, so beautiful," he whispered as he bent his head. The light stroking pressure of his fingertips was soon replaced by the swirling movement of his tongue.

He didn't want to rush things. Gently, Eli took Chloe in his arms, thrilling to the feel of her naked breasts against his bare chest. Her long hair fell over his shoulder like a scented midnight cloud.

He eased the sundress from her hips until the fabric fell with a whisper to the deck, leaving only a scant band of silk underwear. He caught them in his thumbs and inched them over the smooth rounded curve of her bottom.

Without warning, Chloe coaxed the waistband of his jogging shorts off his hips and, bending, she forced the brief band of blue nylon over his thighs. When his shorts slipped down his legs, he stepped out of them.

When she smoothed her palms over his bare buttocks, he reveled in her pleasured gasp. Their hands began to travel the shadowed valleys and seductive planes of one another's bodies.

"Chloe." Eli interrupted the silence long moments later. "Is it time to say 'everybody into the pool'?"

With her courage bolstered by the cloak of near darkness and by her desire to be familiar with the outer beauty of this man, she dared to speak her true feelings.

"Tonight I'm drawn toward fire more than water."

"You want to go back inside?"

"I want to make love to you." She surprised herself when she had no difficulty saying it. "And I want you to make love to me. Tonight. Here. Now."

He placed an arm beneath her knees and lifted her high against his chest. She laughed softly as her head fell against his shoulder. Eli echoed her response, then bent his head to capture her smile with his lips.

"I hope you'll find this," he whispered, setting her

gently on the futon's padding, "your desired destination."

"My destination is to be in your arms, Eli." She sat up and placed her hands on his shoulders.

He found himself unable to resist reaching out and caressing her cheek, touching a finger to the edge of her mouth. The candles surrounding them wavered, casting areas of soft golden light and bronzed shadows over her full high breasts and willowy waist. Areas of light and shadow Eli longed to explore.

He bent to kiss her softly. Then he stood up fully, reaching over to move a candle closer. Chloe continued watching him, filled with wonder as the flickering flames illuminated the body she had all but memorized with her fingertips. His broad powerful shoulders tapered to a narrow waist, slim hips, muscular thighs.

She saw the hunger in his eyes, saw the same hunger reflected in his body. Chloe felt a ripple of desire knowing she had aroused Eli to such a state.

He lay down beside her, enfolding her in his arms, cradling her tenderly against his chest. As he closed his eyes, the memory of the afternoon jarred with the reality of the moment. Not the eroticism of the publicity photos—the vision of Chloe bathed in candlelight and shadows overpowered the need for additional stimuli—it was the impact of discovering Chloe was exalted by some as a sexual symbol.

This woman in his arms was the real Chloe, as only he could know her. Smiling, laughing, teasing, wanting him. *Tonight. Here. Now.*

The Wilde Kingdom

Gently he brushed her hair back from her forehead. Her eyes appeared larger, more luminous, watchful; but the shadow of vulnerability was gone tonight.

He wrapped one hand in the cloud of her ebony hair and, with the other, began once again the sensual journey of his fingertips over the planes of her body. He paused to whisper endearments, to describe his reaction to her perfection, to kiss her with renewed desire and melting tenderness.

She followed, stroking her nails the length of his back, smoothing the pads of her fingertips over his buttocks and the backs of his thighs, trailing torment and pleasure. When her fingers curled intimately around his warm satiny hardness, Chloe was delighted with his breathless entreaty.

His fingers skimmed her upper thighs, then edged slowly into the dark triangle of curls at the juncture of her legs. She moaned against his intimate possession, then arched her hips against the gentle rhythmic motions of his hand.

"Eli," she cried out breathlessly. She wanted to tell him he was the fire she sought, the heat that made her soul dance upward, but words failed her. She clasped and unclasped the fabric beneath her with her fingertips and found she could only cry his name as she strained against the gathering pleasure. "Oh, now. Please, love me now, Eli. I want you."

Moving over her, he entered her firmly, lovingly, completely. Her hips rose up to cradle him, to meet his thrusts and surround him with her feminine warmth.

She was mesmerized by the sight of him moving over her, the private man sharing her private world.

Chloe blinked against the blur of a hundred candles, their flames doubling and fusing as she lost the last vestige of control and felt the waves of passion peak and crest within.

When he felt her begin to contract convulsively around him, Eli allowed the pleasure of his own release. Plunging through a vision of clouds and rain, he found the flames he sought and called her name.

The following morning, Chloe awoke to the muffled cries of ducklings. Disoriented, she tried to move in the direction of the sound and was startled to discover her backside curled intimately against a large male body.

"It's still early." Eli's words were a warm wind against her shoulder. With his hand he pulled her closer in their spoonlike position. "After last night I think we're entitled to sleep in."

"I thought I heard the ducks. The last thing I remember is—Eli, are we in my bed or yours?" she asked, embarrassed by her sleep-drugged state. She tried to separate and sort the events of the previous night but they ran together in her mind like a watercolor . . . making love on the futon and talking in the hot tub and drying in front of the fireplace and carrying candles up the stairs to a four-poster bed so like her own in the cottage and making love so very slowly . . .

"We're in my bed. You did hear ducks. They're

safe in my bathroom—well fed and staying warm in their brooder. And don't worry. Your status as their mother is perfectly safe." His hand traced the line of her body from waist to knee. "They knew instantly that I was an impostor. Not only did they cry, they hid in the corner of the brooder and refused to look at me. Believe me, there's no one quite like you, Chloe."

When she turned onto her back and looked into his face, Eli smiled and brushed the hair back from her eyes.

She was struck by his rugged handsome features. The images from yesterday's experiment would not shake loose. The erotic photos. The sophisticated, cultured man. Whom had she made love to last night? Who lay beside her now? Whom was she slowly falling in love with?

"You look puzzled. The sun is coming up, Chloe. Can you see where you are now?" he asked.

"Yes, of course. We're in your room." She hesitated to mention her qualms. "I-I'm just having these crazy thoughts about what's happened to us. I can't help wondering if opening those packages from New York was like opening Pandora's box."

Eli sighed. "There's nothing wrong with being more aware of each other's career accomplishments."

"But it's more than that. We both have public personas. Last night—"

"What about last night, Chloe?"

"You mentioned the lingerie spread—that photo of me in the red teddy. That's a side of me you didn't know about before. It had to have an effect on you or you wouldn't have mentioned it. And I, well—and all those earthy pictures of you in the rain forest . . . it's the same thing."

"What same thing?"

"I can't help wondering who I made love to, Eli."

He grew quiet for a moment. "You thought I was slipping in and out of personas? I'm not sure if I even know how to do that. I'm one person who occasionally appears in public." He teased the coverlet down, exposing her breasts to his view. "But when you're in my arms, Chloe, I'm thinking of you. You're an audience of one."

"I'm not accusing you of switching back and forth. Do you understand why I'm feeling confused? The confusion is here—" She sighed and pointed to her head. "I had trouble remembering you as I knew you before the package arrived."

"Let me reach under your pillow, Chloe, and we'll see if there's something there that will refresh your memory."

Eli slipped his hand beneath her pillow. "Close your eyes," he said in a whisper, "and relax."

With a patient smile, she closed her eyes. When she attempted to pull the sheet back up over her breasts, his hand intercepted. Then Chloe was startled by the cool feel of metal in the valley between her breasts.

Opening her eyes, she found a tiny wishbone made of gold lying on her chest. Its finely sculpted edges captured the diffused morning sunlight and seemed to glow. Sitting up, she lifted it into her palm and stared, entranced by the simple beauty of it.

"Oh, it's exquisite, Eli." She searched for the right words. "I really don't know what to say."

"Let me put it around your neck." Eli lifted the ends of the black satin cord, placed the necklace around her throat, and fastened the gold clasp.

"It's our wishbone, from the day of the picnic. When you wished joy for me." She looked down and shook her head in disbelief. "Oh, Eli, thank you. It's so personal." She put her arms around his neck.

He lay back against his pillow and pulled her down across her chest. "I put a special kind of magic in there for you because I want all your wishes to come true, Chloe."

"Every wish?"

"Anything within reason."

"Is making love again within reason?"

Chapter 10

AFTERNOON SUN CUT through the alder branches overhead, creating sparkling patterns on the waist-high water in the stream outside the cottage. If anyone had suggested a year ago she'd be spending a summer afternoon sitting in water coaching baby ducks in the art of swimming, Chloe would have laughed in disbelief.

On this July afternoon, she was simply laughing at her predicament. The three-week-old ducklings had her fully trained to respond with a call note to their penetrating piping that signaled duckling distress.

The past week had been hectic. Her five charges had demanded daily outings from their life in the brooder. The outings immediately increased the odds for duckling distress by five hundred percent. There had been changes in their diet, feeding schedule, and play patterns. And there'd been a dramatic increase in the number of times the little ducks cried wolf.

Eli had assisted with the first field trip to the swimming hole, nailing up chicken wire to keep the small ducks from floating downstream. Even then, Eli and Chloe had carried vegetable strainers and fishing nets in case an emergency rescue was necessary.

"All right, gang!" Chloe pulled herself out of the water, her scant swimsuit dripping down on the ducklings, bringing the small flock to immediate attention. "We're going to climb out of the water and up the bank and sit in the sun to dry off. Ready?"

Moses uttered a toneless baritone chirp and took off ahead of Chloe, waddling up the muddy bank before she could get a handhold. "You're looking at five demerits, Moses!" In her attempt to capture the runaway, she slipped and fell back into the water.

Swearing softly, she recovered and quickly counted the remaining flock of four while Moses mocked her from the upper bank. "You're just auditioning for the role of villain in my Sunday strip, aren't you?"

"Adding new characters to 'The Wilde Kingdom'?" a strangely familiar male voice asked from the footbridge over the stream. Shading her eyes, Chloe glimpsed a tall blond figure in a summer sports coat, slacks, and tie.

"Eli, I can't believe you're asking silly questions when I need help catching Moses." She rose, dripping once again, from the stream and proceeded up the muddy bank. "Are you going into town? I haven't seen you with so many clothes on since the night we played strip poker and you cheated."

Her laughter made her slip backward, but she quickly regained her composure. As she reached the path, her attention was riveted on Moses, who cried shrilly and struggled in a pair of large male hands. Hands without rings. Hands that did not belong to Eli. She looked up with trepidation, then froze in horror.

"You're not Eli."

"I sort of wish I was. I'm sorry, I should have announced myself, Ms. Wilde." The stranger seemed to be enjoying her discomfort. "We're frequently confused but I'm Eli's brother, Gabe, of course."

"Of course. You're Gabe Kellerman. Good Lord, you're the one who laid the eggs—excuse me—who left the eggs in the cottage." She reached out to take the shrieking Moses from Gabe's hands. The rest of the flock chimed in as soon as they spotted the stranger in their midst.

"Eli asked me to stop in and get to know the ducks." Gabe raised his voice as the crying increased. "I'll be—I said I'll be watching the ducks the weekend after next when the two of you go into Seattle for his new show! Do they always cry like this?"

"Only when they lose sight of my face!"

"That might present problems for me if you're gone!"

"No problem!" Chloe shouted. "Eli stuck pictures of me in the brooder and around the cottage! Please, come over to the blanket on the grass! I can sit down where they'll see me and they need to dry off in the sun before they go back inside!"

"Ms. Wilde—"

"Please call me Chloe!" Grabbing a beach towel from the grass beside the blanket, she wrapped it around her wet bikini. The man must think her daft—talking about strip poker, chasing ducks, and talking about demerits in a half-naked state, blathering on about how the ducklings needed to see her face! First impressions were lasting impressions.

To make matters worse, he worked for a newspaper. Chloe wondered if a photographer was hiding in the bushes.

"Perhaps you should sit down." Gabe suggested. "To quiet the ducks."

"Of course." She lowered herself to the blanket as gracefully as possible, praying she wouldn't sit on a member of her flock. As the ducks huddled around her, she picked up a lump of clay from her basket and began shaping it. "You're a reporter, right?"

"I'm an editor for the Olympic City paper, and I write mystery novels."

Terrific, Chloe thought. A snoop and a sleuth rolled into one neat package. A package that looked a great deal like Eli. But for some reason, she wasn't ready to extend her trust. How much had Eli told his brother? Did Gabe know about her creative block?

"Look, I didn't mean to embarrass you or invade your privacy, Chloe. Actually, I've been a big fan of yours since the early days of 'The Wilde Kingdom.'"

"Did Eli tell you about the night the eggs hatched?"

The Wilde Kingdom

"Uh, not really. I mean, not in detail. Do you actually swim with the ducks or do you—"

"That's why I mentioned the hatching. The ducklings imprinted on me that night. They think I'm their mother." Chloe briefly described the daily routine of a surrogate duck mother to Gabe. "But they shouldn't really be a problem for you. The ducks stay in the brooder much of the time now, but they'll be five weeks old by the time we go to Seattle. I'll have their fenced pen completed. The people over at Camden Farm have ducks and they're giving me pointers. Oh, I should introduce them by name."

Gabe Kellerman simply nodded as she pointed out Ping, Pong, Waddles, Daffy, and Moses. Chloe was perturbed. He seemed more interested in ogling her than learning how to deal with young ducklings.

"It surprises me to see you working in clay." Gabe switched the subject again. "That's Bar-B-Cue the Cow you're shaping, isn't it?"

Chloe looked down at the three-dimensional form of her beloved friend. Reaching up, she touched the golden wishbone at her throat. She made a silent request for a miracle that would dismiss this annoying man. *Rescue me now, Bar-B-Cue.*

Seconds later Moses charged Gabe's hand, grabbing the tip of the man's forefinger in his small beak.

"Ow!" Gabe reacted with a cry of pain. "Let go! Let go! Does this duck have teeth? I swear it must be part piranha."

Moses opened his beak, released his captive, and waddled back to Chloe's side.

"You're bleeding, Gabe." Chloe tried to sound concerned. "Perhaps you should go to the big house and take care of your bite. And why don't I write down a list of everything you need to know about the ducklings for next weekend? All right?" Chloe had yet to take her hand off the wishbone at her throat.

"I still wish you'd stopped by here first, Gabe, instead of dropping in unannounced at the cottage." Eli paced the kitchen angrily while his brother ran water over his forefinger. "I guaranteed Chloe privacy. I can't believe you grilled her with questions—"

"I didn't say I grilled her. I asked a few simple questions and told her I was a fan. No big deal." Gabe turned the water off and inspected his finger warily. "Can you get rabies from a duck bite?"

"I wouldn't worry. You're probably immune to rabies. I'm more concerned about what Moses might catch from you."

"Testy, aren't we, big brother?" Gabe poured himself a cup of coffee and leaned against the counter. "You don't want me snooping around here because she's gotten under your skin, am I right?"

"What makes you think there's something going on?"

"I was standing on the footbridge and she mistook me for you. Said she hadn't seen you wearing so many clothes since you cheated at strip poker."

"Oh, Lord."

"You know, Chloe's everything I thought she'd be. Beautiful, evasive, kooky, eccentric, and sexier than hell." Gabe shook his head. "She lives up to her image and then some. I just didn't figure anything would happen between the two of you. It's like Humphrey Bogart meets "I Love Lucy" on *The African Queen*."

"Lucy? I think you're a poor judge of character, Gabe. Chloe is more of a Lauren Bacall than you realize."

"Interesting. Who started it?"

"Who *started* it?"

"Yeah, did you just fall into each other's arms as soon as she arrived?"

"As a matter of fact, we did. In a treetop, no less."

"Sounds appropriate for your woodsman image." Gabe took a reporter's pad out of the inside pocket of his jacket. "Mind if I take notes?"

"Yes, I mind." Eli took the pad from his brother and set it on the counter. "You've seen nothing and heard nothing, got it?"

"This would make an amazing story, Eli."

"Followed immediately by your amazing funeral. Do you think the world would mourn the loss of a rabid mystery writer?"

"So you *can* catch rabies from ducks? If Moses begins exhibiting unusual behavior, you'll let me know, won't you?"

"The little runt has exhibited unusual behavior since he hatched. On a more serious note, Gabe—" Eli quickly ended the repartee with his brother. "Chloe is hardly kooky. She's a warm, intelligent, sensitive woman—"

"Whose fans are clamoring to get her back."

"What?"

"You haven't read the papers? People claim they're having 'Wilde Kingdom' withdrawal symptoms. They're addicted to Chloe's strip and say it's unfair to quit cold turkey. It's gotten a lot of press. They want her back immediately."

"You're joking."

"At first I thought it was a tongue-in-cheek campaign cooked up by her syndicate or some public-relations jerk, but it seems to be happening around the country. She's a phenomenon, Eli." Gabe gestured dramatically with his hands. "If you knew anything about popular culture, you'd understand the importance of cartoon characters!"

"Listen to yourself, Gabe. And you're calling Chloe a kook?"

"I didn't come here to argue."

"No, I think you came here to snoop."

"Eli, you're just so unaware of how a comic strip can become a national fixation—"

"I've got news for you, brother. I'm no longer uninformed when it comes to Chloe Wilde or her precious 'Kingdom.' I've seen every photo ever taken of her, studied every cartoon, and I've read all the interviews and articles. I know the full extent of her popularity, but more importantly, I've gotten to know the person." Eli looked away, afraid his feelings would be too evident. He paused to search for the right words. "She doesn't need any additional pressure right now. Do me a favor and don't mention any of this hype about fan withdrawal to Chloe."

"You're renting a cottage to the woman, Eli. It sounds like you want to build a moat and—well, I just don't remember you being this overprotective with Vanessa."

Gabe was right. Chloe brought the protective streak out in him. The day after they'd made love for the first time, he'd begun taking black-and-white photos of Chloe at her request. She'd turned the camera on him a few times as well. She wanted mementos of her sabbatical, photos taken of her private self, posing with Chomp and the ducklings, grocery shopping in Two Corners, walking through meadows, visiting the artists' colony next door on the Camden Farm, sitting by the fireplace and making clay figures.

He recalled the first set of prints developed by a photographer at Camden. Her sleepy eyes stared out at him, honest, open, unguarded.

"Chloe's very vulnerable, Gabe," he attempted to answer his brother's question. "It takes a lot of extra effort for her to trust people."

"Bull. The woman I just met gave me the impression she could be formidable. She's successful and wealthy and she's got the press in her pocket. She shouldn't have a care in the world."

"You're right, Gabe. Chloe *shouldn't* have a care in the world. The truth is, she has some overwhelming concerns. I just hope you and the people like you don't become another concern."

* * *

"Chloe, you're being silly. The cottage is too small." Eli stood in the doorway shaking his head. "You need more room. I have a huge house with four empty bedrooms, and rooms I never use. Why aren't you listening?"

"Because I'm afraid, Eli." Chloe shrugged her shoulders and looked out her kitchen window at the pasture beyond. "If I move all my projects over to your house and something happens between us to create bad feelings, things would be stickier. A complicated situation might hurt the progress I've made on my creative block."

"But look at this place. An artist can't work in the midst of chaos. There's clay or clay figures on every surface." He threw up his hands and pointed to a cluttered wall. "You—you have a sheet of paper running from the kitchen to the bedroom. Chomp doesn't even have room to turn around in here, the poor dog!"

Chloe looked out the window at Chomp, running free in the meadow with the five other Kellerman dogs and two frisky canines from Camden Farm.

"I don't think Chomp is concerned about space right now." She laughed and turned in Eli's arms to face him. "The sheet of paper you're complaining about is a timeline of 'The Wilde Kingdom.' I went back to the beginning and wrote down all the changes Bar-B-Cue and her colleagues have gone through. I needed to have a sense of where I've been to know where I'm going. You know, something tangible to measure how my characters have changed, how Bar-B-Cue's grown—how I've grown."

"Makes sense. I'm sorry to blather on about neatness. Don't listen to me. You know I'm something of a perfectionist. A place for everything and everything in its place."

"Sounds boring. I do like a little bit of clutter . . . and lots of spontaneity. Believe me, it helps to have the ducks in a the pen now. Everything's coming together, Eli, like you said it would. I know my system's not orderly or neat, but it's working."

She looked up into his blue eyes and saw caring and concern reflected in their depths. "I didn't plan to tell you so soon, Mr. Kellerman, but something extraordinary happened this morning."

"I thought you went over to Camden Farm to work on your 'animal familiarization project.'"

"Why do you always use that teasing tone when we talk about my project?" Chloe tickled Eli around the ribs. "Do you think my fear of animals is a laughing matter?"

"You know better. I just get a kick out of picturing you edging closer and closer to a cow."

Chloe moved out of his arms. "I'm serious. I was over at Camden Farm this morning. After viewing the cows and horses I talked to one of the residents about how to improve the pen I built for the ducks and *suddenly* I had this urge . . . this crazy urge to draw."

"To draw what?"

"Bar-B-Cue, but there was this twist that came to mind. Promise not to laugh?"

"I promise."

"I wanted my supercow to have a baby—Baby Short Ribs. When I got back to the cottage I started sketching out this new character. I was actually excited about it, Eli. But then I looked at the timeline and I thought about my motivation and how the change would affect the strip. Maybe I was motivated by my own wish for stability."

"You're not discouraged, are you?"

"No, no. I was proud I didn't jump at the first idea that popped into my head. And I kept on drawing. Just bits and pieces, nothing solid, Eli. But what I did sketch out looked slightly different. My style has changed, but not in a way I can define. And I don't want to show you anything. Not just yet. I don't want criticism or analysis or pressure."

"Then what can I do to help?"

"Just be who you are, Eli." She was startled by her own words. Did she really know where the private Eli ended and the public Eli began? Would attending the gala opening of his Seattle show really give her the insight she needed?

Chloe ran her finger over the silver dragon on his chest. *Ch'i.* She recalled the moment he spoke the name he'd given the talisman. Bathed in the afterglow of lovemaking, they were talking of things private and profound. Laughing softly. When she asked about the dragon, she was surprised to learn Eli had made the whimsical creature in his early years as a sculptor and designer.

As he told her about his reasons for moving away from sculpting animals to realistic nature motifs, she sensed a change in him. A shift to the public man who depended on his fine art training.

In that moment, she'd felt as though she'd lost a part of him. In her mind, the images had yet to merge. Now as she touched the dragon and looked up into Eli's features, she experienced again the doubt of that earlier moment.

Did she really know him? Which image was she falling in love with? The same question that had haunted her continued to move through the labyrinth of her heart.

Chapter 11

FROM HER HIDING place in one of the boutique's dressing rooms, Chloe still heard faint echoes of the voices that had greeted her entrance to the showing. She cringed against the memory.

"Chloe Wilde! This is a surprise!"

"I've really missed your comic strip."

"Love your wishbone necklace. I always thought you must be a fan of Elijah Kellerman's work. What did you think of his—"

"How's your sabbatical coming along? Hadn't it been at least six weeks now?"

"You look so tanned and rested. I wish I could vacation for three months."

"You look great in that color. What brought you to Eli's showing?"

She'd dodged the more direct questions as graciously as possible with her usual blend of humor and counterquestioning. She'd seen her share of cocktail parties, art openings, literary events, and awards banquets. It was her custom to retreat, relax, and regroup before resuming the role of fun-loving cartoonist.

Chloe finished her glass of champagne, stood up, glanced over the door of the dressing room, and made a flawless exit back into the milling crowd of well-dressed patrons.

Events such as this always challenged her ability to play chameleon. Her secrets were simple. Keep 'em laughing, keep their eyes on your dress and hair and, if possible your shoes, and keep moving around the room.

But tonight was different. It was Eli's long-awaited Seattle showing, held at one of the most exclusive boutiques in the city. She didn't want to think about avoiding or manipulating those who approached her. Chloe wanted to feel like a part of crowd. One of many. Just another patron enjoying the singular beauty of Eli's work.

She made her way closer, studying him from a distance. With his tall muscular frame, he looked dramatically elegant in his white silk suit and burgundy shirt.

Fresh flowers in crystal vases, subdued lighting, a cellist playing softly in the corner—Chloe slowly became aware of individual details that lent to the magic of the evening. But her attention returned again

The Wilde Kingdom   141

and again to the man in white capturing and holding the light, holding the magic for her.

The erotic posters of Eli she had become so familiar with over the past month hung in frames about the boutique. Two women stood in front of the rain forest pose, discussing the Kellerman anatomy in frank, approving tones.

Chloe felt a warm blush spread up her throat and face as they spoke. When had she become such a part of Eli's life? When had she developed these protective feelings about his image?

Their emotions were entangled in some inexplicable way. She hesitated to allow the "L" word to become a part of her vocabulary, verbal or mental. In thirty years of living, she could not remember hearing anyone say "I love you." As a child, she could only imagine the wonder of it. Perhaps it was best, she often consoled herself at that age. Since her early years had been a series of traumatic partings, she could only imagine that the "L" word would have complicated matters.

And so it was that love mingled with a lightning bolt had become the source of Bar-B-Cue the Cow's special powers. The bovine's ability to love others without prejudgment was the secret to her continuing strength. Chloe wondered if she had mentioned this love to Eli when he asked about the supercow's origins.

She moved away from the posters, making small talk as she placed smoked salmon, brie, and grapes on a plate. Chloe watched as a female patron approached

Eli with a question about arranging two designs to work together. Smiling, chatting amicably, Eli positioned the woman in front of a mirror, slipped the first piece, a silver cluster of thimbleberries, around her neck. Patiently he moved the second necklace, a grouping of leaves, up and down, attempting to create a balance.

"It's like searching for the right harmony," he explained candidly. "You might like each of these individually but, together, I can't really find the right *tune*, so to say." Then, drawing back, he studied the woman's face more intently.

"You have such delicate features, Irene," he continued. "If you want a grouping of two, I can still suggest combining the thimbleberries with the Queen Anne's lace you purchased last year, or looking at this year's vinework."

"Vines? As long as they don't remind me of the problem I'm having with morning glories in my garden," the woman chided good-naturedly.

Seconds later, Chloe caught Eli's glance and returned his fleeting smile. She paused in midstride to contemplate the change in him. The aloofness she'd seen in the posters was there, but she couldn't define the source. His eyes? The set of his mouth? How could a man be aloof yet exude a warm, personal touch? It was as if part of his final satisfaction as an artist was to see that the wearer took full advantage of the versatility of his designs.

She moved closer to the crowded counter, relishing the feeling of being just another patron perusing the shimmering silver jewelry. She and Eli had agreed before arriving at the boutique that it would be best to keep their relationship secret. It would be too easy for media people to spot the connection between her sabbatical and Eli's remote location. Both wanted to avoid the unwelcome visitors who might disrupt their lives.

As she turned to accept another glass of champagne, the hauntingly sad yet beautiful music drew her attention past the counters, past the crowds to the lovely cellist in the corner. And there beside the young woman was a pedestal that seemed set apart, displaying a delicate sculpted seashell. She walked toward it, balancing her drink in her hand.

Eli had been watching for glimpses of Chloe all evening. She'd appeared unnerved by the overwhelming welcome she'd received when she first entered the boutique, but she recovered quickly and graciously.

This was his first opportunity to observe her in a crowd. Chloe's purple dress, cut with a deep V front and a long flowing skirt, made it easy to find her no matter how brief the glance. She was stunning. In a large room filled with beautiful bejeweled women dressed in haute couture, Chloe was a precious jewel unto herself.

She showed none of the signs of insecurity he had anticipated. Her confident stance was coupled with direct eye contact. Her smile was warm if not contagious.

During the past six weeks, he'd come to know the strength and determination of the woman behind the vulnerable eyes. In her own point of view, she had not been unlucky, she had been challenged early in life. Once again, this time in the midst of comfort and financial security, she had been challenged by a creative block that forced her to reevaluate the direction of her life.

When she parted from the crowd, he saw the opportunity to move toward her without drawing attention. As he slipped behind the clerks attending the counters, Eli watched Chloe put down her champagne and pick up his sculpture of a seashell. With childlike abandon, she lifted the delicate shell to her ear, closed her eyes, and smiled to herself.

"What do you hear?" he asked, leaning close.

"It's what I *don't* hear." She opened her eyes slowly, seemingly unaware of the crowded room or the cellist who smiled in their direction. "The blessed sound of silence, Eli. No crying ducks."

"Let me put an ocean in there for you," he whispered.

"Which ocean?"

"The South Pacific. Somewhere near Bali Hai. At sunset."

She lifted the shell back up to her ear. "You're a man of many skills, Mr. Kellerman."

"I don't do oceans for just anyone. You're pretty special too. I'd kiss you right now but we agreed to keep things quiet."

"Then kiss me quiet."

"That, my lady, is impossible." He picked up the glass of champagne she'd set down. "Not only is your face one of the most recognizable in this room, but you look stunning tonight. Conspicuously stunning. And every cell in my body knows it."

"That's my drink you just picked up."

"I know. I'll kiss the lip of the champagne glass *quietly* before I go back to my grueling work."

"And I'm supposed to pick it up and swoon?" she asked with a laugh.

"Be nice, Chloe," he teased, "or I'll take back my ocean."

"Oooh! I never realized you had this cruel streak."

"I don't," he said quickly, smiling as he stepped back in the direction of the counter. "I'll take away the ocean and offer you the moon . . . tonight when we're alone in your condo."

"Your home reflects the Chloe Wilde I know so well," Eli commented after she began taking him on a leisurely tour of suite 1801. "Your trademarks are here. Bright colors, whimsical wildlife, good taste."

Beginning in the foyer, there were wall graphics of birds, reptiles, and animals, assembling in twos as if preparing to board Noah's ark. As they progressed through the rooms, other duos of animals emerged from windows and skylights and kitchen cabinets to join the long continuous line. Where did it end? he wondered.

"You'd be surprised at how many people follow the wild kingdom all the way to my bedroom."

"Are you sure you don't want to rephrase that remark?"

"It's true, Eli. They get caught up in the wall graphic and end up pulling back my shower curtain to find out—" She stood in a doorway, looked at him, and paused. "I think I'll make you wait until later to conclude this tour. You have a gleam in your eye that makes me think—"

"I demand to see the conclusion. I can't believe all this"—he gestured toward the colorful pictures of animals marching in twos—"ends in your private bath."

"All right. Follow me." She walked through the doorway into a spacious bedroom. The line of animals that had begun as a trickle in the foyer and grew throughout the kitchen, living room, and dining room, blossomed in the bedroom.

Immediately Eli noted the change in ambiance. The mood was one of tenderness and caring here. Giant pandas, elephants, tigers, birds, turtles, armadillos, butterflies, mice, and rabbits frolicking playfully, kissing, hugging, and painted in a variety of intimate poses.

"I'm not sure—" He turned to Chloe. "It's not blatant but some of them look as thought they might be making love!"

"The designer and I thought it appropriate for the bedroom. Of course, we selected some prints of men and women to hang on the walls—just to acknowledge the human race."

"Nice. Very nice." Eli moved closer to the wall and began inspecting the paintings at closer range. He passed by one of the windows offering a panoramic view of Seattle. "Does anyone even notice the view?"

"I rarely get visitors, Eli."

"Well, this visitor is impressed." He took his time taking in all the detail. "Who was the painter?"

"There was a team of artists. The bedroom took the longest time to coordinate because my wishes were specific and, frankly, they'd never had an order of that nature. I stopped in every day during the process and felt like I was intruding on some intimate ritual. A woman named Margie did most of the work."

"Did you pick up a paintbrush and lend a hand, Chloe?"

"See the two cows near the closet? Margie let me paint in the eyes. I was tempted to paint eyes that rolled but I chose a *contented* look in the end."

"Tasteful, Chloe. I like this. Honestly. I like it a lot." Eli slipped off his white jacket and laid it on the bed. "I'm almost afraid to admit this but I find this room incredibly erotic."

"You're brave. I'm sure a lot of people feel that way but they're not willing to admit it out loud. Ready to see the finale?"

She opened the double doors to the bathroom. The floor, ceiling, and walls were a lush green garden populated with harmonious scenes of animals of different species working, playing, singing, dancing, and planting flowers together.

A plush green carpet bordered with colorful flowers took precedence in the center of the room. A vanity sat in a well-lit alcove where wildlife helped one another with makeup and hairstyling.

"Your shower curtain is amazing." Eli touched a finger to the raised imprint of a small red rose. "These feel like—are these real flowers?"

"Uh-huh. Dried and pressed between two clear sheets of vinyl. The finale I promised you is behind here." With a smile, Chloe pulled the shower curtain back, exposing a large sunken tub.

Eli released the air in his lungs slowly. The tub was surrounded by a tile mural with a background of azure blue. Light from the building opposite shone through the skylight overhead.

"The lion lies down with the lamb. I like the simplicity," Eli said at last. "You must spend hours in here just letting your mind float from animal to animal."

"I've been such a workaholic. I'm not sure if I've ever really taken the time to appreciate what I have. *Yet*. But all this has new meaning for me now, Eli." Chloe walked back into the bedroom.

"How's that?"

"I'm slowly overcoming my fear of animals. I know these are not accurate depictions of ferocious beasts but, right now, these creatures look brand new to me."

"Because of the sabbatical?"

"Because of you, Eli. And maybe because I made an effort to change the way I've felt all these years. You made it easier for me. Having to deal with five newly hatched ducklings helped. And good ol' Chomp, of course."

"Of course." He pulled her into his arms. "You

look a little overwhelmed. How does it feel to be back?"

"This is the first time I've ever been gone for so long. Six weeks. I won't really know until I see my studio."

"Should we check it out?"

"No, that's private, Eli. I'll deal with it later. Right now—" Her eyes darted quickly to the intimate scenes on the wall.

"Don't tell me, Ms. Wilde. Do I bring out the animal in you or is it the artwork?"

"You." She growled seductively and laughed. He captured her laughter with a tender kiss, then bent to kiss one exposed shoulder.

"Did I tell you I love this dress?" His hands slipped down her back and cupped her rounded derriere. "Chloe?" he raised his brows and sought her gaze. "Are you wearing—" His hands snaked under the skirt of her dress and skimmed up her thighs. "Hmmmm." Eli smiled and groaned against her neck. "How did you know I love garters and French lace?"

"You said you liked the photo of me in the red teddy. I couldn't buy lingerie during our weekly trips to Two Corners—"

"Of course not. You were posing as a respectable woman shopping with a semirespectable man." He was unzipping the back of the purple dress with a slow even stroke.

"Eli!"

"Blame it on the cuddly animals on the walls."

"You're trying to pull my dress off!"

"And you're not trying to stop me. What were you saying about lingerie in Two Corners?"

"I was going to say . . ." Her voice grew muffled as he continued pulling the dress over her head. ". . . I knew about a little lingerie shop here in Seattle, so this afternoon while you were making arrangements for tonight's gala event . . ."

"Dear Lord." Eli let the purple dress fall in a silken whisper to the floor. He took in the sight of Chloe in red teddy, matching red garters, and sheer black nylons.

She laughed and stepped back. "While you're standing there thinking less than respectable thoughts, Mr. Kellerman, I wonder if you know how much I love suspenders on men?" Leaning forward slightly, she looped a finger under one strap and bean teasing it from his shoulder. "Two can play at this game."

"Play on." Eli moved closer. "Do you realize how many pairs of eyes are watching us?"

"Contented eyes."

"You don't find it unnerving?"

"We're in my home now, Eli. It's time you got acquainted with the *real* Wilde kingdom."

A few hours later, Chloe held her breath as she opened the door to her studio. Light from the hall lamp illuminated a portion of the room. As she stood in the doorway staring at the objects cast half in shadow, half in light, she saw the analogy to her creative block.

There were the old fears, half-hidden in shadow,

she had yet to confront. She smiled slightly as she thought of the progress she'd made, the light shed on old secrets, old fears that had been unraveled and made harmless by her own examination.

Wrapping her Chinese robe tightly around her body, she stepped cautiously toward her drawing table and switched on the adjustable overhead lamp. Positioned squarely in the center of her working space was the blank Bristol board she'd confronted on the morning of her thirtieth birthday two months ago.

It was less intimidating now.

Since she'd entered the condo with Eli late last evening, Chloe hadn't been able to shake the feeling that someone other than her housekeeper had come in and rearranged her furniture, changed the intensity of the lighting, and altered the size of every room.

After close scrutiny, she concluded everything was as she'd left it. Which meant she had to look closer—at the changes she'd gone through while living in Eli's cottage. To understand those changes, she felt the need to enter her studio and think about life as it was before her thirtieth birthday.

Still bathed in the afterglow of their lovemaking, she found it hard to reflect on life before Eli. Her home on the eighteenth floor was vibrant, colorful, uniquely hers. But in many ways life in these rooms had been more remote than living on Eli's secluded farm.

Living alone. Working alone. She'd called it creative solitude, but the memory of sleepness nights returned. She'd been haunted by thoughts that her life might be limited by unseen boundaries much like the lives of her characters were limited by the enclosed frame of her comic strip. She'd closed her world off at some point, unable to trust those people who might befriend her because of her celebrated public image.

Her old fears seemed foolish now. Anything was possible. Trusting Eli had been instinctual, but she'd learned to extend her trust further and further daily.

Chloe sat down at the drawing table and touched a finger to the pristine Bristol board in front of her. Raising her head, she stared out her large window at the lights of Seattle's harbor and Elliot Bay. Above the scene in the clear summer sky, there hung a crescent moon.

Eli had promised to give her the moon . . . What had he meant by that remark?

Mesmerized, she let her thoughts float freely, barely skimming the surface of her languid mood. Her hand moved up to the golden wishbone at her throat.

"If fishes were wishes . . ." The words came to her in a flutter of loose phrases that fell like meteors across the moonscape of her mind. Effortlessly she picked up a pencil and drew a fish with a troubled face.

"It's eight o'clock in the morning," Eli announced from the open doorway. "How long have you been sitting there?"

"A few hours, but the results are amazing." Chloe made no attempt to disguise the excitement in her voice. "Eli, I'm not really ready to sit down and show you everything, but I have six strips and about fifteen working ideas and two new characters that I need to flesh out and—"

"Fantastic. I'll wait until you're ready to show me. You must be exhausted." He spoke close to her ear. "Want me to massage your shoulders?"

"My shoulders? Uh—I don't think they're tense. I feel—lighter."

"Then I'll make coffee and run out and find something sinfully delicious for your breakfast."

"Thank you," She turned and kissed him softly. "I'm not ignoring you, Eli. It's like the sky opened for me and all this—" She swept her arms wide to indicate the work on the drawing table. "This is the manna I've been waiting for."

"And this"—Eli lifted a velvet-wrapped object from the pocket of his robe—"is the moon I promised you."

As the velvet fell away revealing a sliver of sleek silver, Chloe inhaled sharply. Sitting on her drawing board, atop her sketches, was her crescent moon.

"Does this mean you'll take back my ocean?"

"No, the seashell is in your bedroom, ocean fully restored. I left it under the painting of the cow with the contented eyes.

"Thank you, Eli." Chloe tested the weight of the silver moon in her palm. "This has extra-special meaning to me now."

He watched her for a moment and recognized the struggle of an artist torn between spending time working and spending time with someone she cared about.

"Chloe, why don't I call my brother and see if we can stay in Seattle an extra day. I think it might be important to you."

"But he has his job at the paper and his current novel to work on—I don't want to impose."

"Chloe, that's part of your problem. You don't impose on other people enough. Let me worry about my brother. I'll just tell him you need time to appreciate the new moon from your own window."

Chapter 12

ONE WEEK LATER, Marty Blashfield sat on the love seat opposite Chloe in Eli Kellerman's plush studio, perusing a multitude of "Wilde Kingdom" strips. "Nice, Chloe. Nice. Incredible. Everything here looks great!"

Chloe leaned closer to the coffee table that separated her from her longtime business manager. Though Marty had given them only one day's notice of his short visit, Eli had stepped quickly into the role of gracious host. She'd found it more difficult to welcome Marty warmly.

So much was at stake. On one hand, she didn't want to view Marty's approval of the revised "Wilde Kingdom" as validation of her continued career as a cartoonist. She had to find that validation in her own heart. On the other hand, as one professional to another, she sought her business manager's honest opinion.

"Marty, what do you think about the changes?"

"They're subtle, but we know the public will be looking for them. Critics will be—hey, they'll be critics, right?"

"Right."

"But I didn't fly all the way to the wilds of Washington State to pass judgment on the new look of 'The Wilde Kingdom.' I'm not the expert. You know your characters and you know your style." Marty swept a palm over the artwork on the coffee table. "If you're comfortable with the product, sweetheart, then I'm comfortable."

"I don't usually feel this positive about my work, Marty," she said, choking back a nervous laugh. "I just hope I'm not fooling myself. The only thing I'm really worried about is the reaction of my loyal fans. I really care about those people."

"So do I. We have to care about them." Marty's expression grew serious. "And that's why I'm here. The public, the syndicate, and every card shop and stationery boutique in the country is anxious for the return of your strip."

"Great." She lifted Marty's calendar from the table and flipped a page. "My sabbatical will be over in less than five weeks. We can worry about getting back into a schedule then."

"But there's a problem with that."

"What?"

"Actually, we've got two problems. We both know

it was a hasty decision, taking this sudden and very mysterious sabbatical." Marty stood up and poured another glass of mineral water from the bottle on the cart next to the table.

"Not only did it cause chaos in scheduling for the syndicate, it caused delays in production and distribution of greeting cards, mugs, and such. Plans for twelve new greeting cards were scrapped until further notice." He began a slow steady walk around the studio, stopping to study paintings and prints along the walls. "I know it was a personal emergency that prompted your need to escape, but in the end, we should have planned it more carefully."

In a nutshell, her haste had inconvenienced a number of people. For some strange reason, she wasn't burdening herself with guilt about the matter. Guilt wouldn't change what had already been done.

"What's the second problem, Marty?"

"I don't need to tell you it's customary for a cartoonist to work four weeks ahead of release date, which means I'll take these back to New York"—he took a sip of mineral water—"and the syndicate will have approximately one week to see them before you're locked back into newspaper schedules across the country."

"When I took three months off, I assumed I could stay on the Kellerman farm until the final week then—Marty, how could I be so scatteredbrained? So unprofessional? I completely forgot about the four-week deadline. I didn't think to make arrangements with the syndicate or—"

"It's not the end of the world. But the reality is—*this* is your last week of vacation, Chloe. You'll have to get back into an active schedule."

"What alternative do I have?"

"You can ask for another three months."

"Inconvenience more people, right?" Chloe shook her head and sat back against the cushions, fighting the guilt feelings that pressed in on her. "Taking this time off has made me realize what a people pleaser I am. I really do need to give my own health—mental and physical—a higher priority."

"So what's your decision?"

"Good Lord, Marty. This is my life! Give me a minute to think about it."

"We still have to discuss publicity. I think you should grant a few interviews and talk about your sabbatical. Pose with those cows you showed me next door." He gestured toward the window with his upraised glass. "Get photographs of yourself and a few of the folks from the artist's colony. You might give brief mention to the creative block—people love it when a celebrity overcomes a personal problem. And don't forget Eli Kellerman. He'd be good for more than just a sidebar—"

"Marty!" Chloe stood up and walked toward him. "You make it sound like we're already going to press! I haven't even made a decision yet. What exactly are you suggesting? That I fabricate some idyllic sabbatical for the press?"

"Don't get upset, sweetheart." Marty flashed a smile. "It's not really fabrication."

"I'm tired of you telling me that." She failed to return the smile. "I've listened to you making mincemeat of semantics long enough. Why can't I tell them the truth? That the changes in 'The Wilde Kingdom' reflect the changes in me? That I've taken the time to work through old hurts from my childhood and I've gained insight into why I've always used humor as a defense against real feelings?"

"Chloe, that isn't necessary." Marty set his glass back down on the coffee table and turned his full attention on her. "In fact, it could be downright depressing. Think of it. A cartoonist makes people laugh. You don't want to disillusion your fans. In their eyes, you're glamorous, sexy, zany, carefree, and hilarious."

"And you want me to continue that charade?" Chloe raised her voice and stepped closer. "Marty, look at me. The real me. I'm sensitive and emotional . . . "

She thought of the relationship she'd maintained with Martin Blashfield all these years. He'd encouraged the clowning, the sexist hype. If he'd really known her, he would have realized how much conflict the double persona had brought to her life.

"How can I begin to explain myself to you?" she asked after a long silence.

"You don't have to, Chloe. It's easy to see you've gone through changes. I'm not trying to belittle what you've been through. Thirty is a turning point for a lot of people. I had my own crisis at thirty-eight. Ten years later, I'm just beginning to understand it."

"I don't expect to get a clear picture of everything

all at once, Marty." Chloe leaned back against the stone fireplace where she and Eli had shared so many fires on late summer evenings. *A fire in June.* She recalled the heat of their first lovemaking.

It was early August now and the flames burned brighter, steadier. Eli claimed he drew strength from fire. Through Eli and Chomp and her ducklings, she'd learned to lean on herself, to draw strength from the same inner well that had sustained her through her troubled younger years.

How could she explain her deep feelings for Eli to Marty or to members of the press when she hadn't been able to put them into words for herself? But matters of the heart would have to wait.

At the moment, it was important to convey her professionalism and desire to cooperate to her business manager.

"Marty, exactly how soon do you want me to make a decision about scheduling the first week of 'The Wilde Kingdom'?"

"It would help to have firm plans before I return to New York tomorrow morning."

"I have three weeks of dailies and at least five Sunday releases here on the table. There are rough sketches in the cottage, Marty, and I can—"

At that moment, there was a loud clattering at the French doors that led to the outer deck. Five ducks quacked loudly and beat their bills relentlessly against the lowest panes of glass.

"Excuse me, Marty, They've gotten out of their pen

again!" Chloe move quickly across the studio floor, fearful the glass would shatter from the impact.

The combination soon brought Chomp and the five other Kellerman hounds, who began barking and running back and forth across the deck. Chloe tried to push the French doors open without harming the six-week-old ducks.

"Quiet, Chomp! Poor duckies. In their little eyes, I'm their mother." She made a brief attempt to explain the imprinting to Marty for the sixth time in less than twenty-four hours.

"Are you trying to get out or let them in?" he shouted over the cacophony.

"I might as well let them in so they won't be frightened by the dogs." She managed to open the door one duck width. The ducks ran in one at a time, then immediately looked up at Chloe, elongating their necks as they cried in distress. Out on the deck, Chomp and friends pushed their noses against the French doors and barked their displeasure.

One lone duck rushed at the closed door, quacking in short baritone notes at the canines who only intensified their barking.

"Moses!" Chloe called toward the youngest, smartest, and boldest of her charges. No doubt, he had orchestrated the escape from the pen and led the search for "Mother."

"Need a little help with your flock, Reverend Wilde?"

Chloe turned toward the workshop at the sound of Eli's deep, rich laughter.

"Eli! I didn't mean to let them into your studio."

"Don't worry, no damage done!" he shouted over the incessant barking. He then assured her with his easy smile. "I'll go out on the deck and get the dogs under control so you can handcuff these hardened criminals and herd them out of here. I know you and Marty have business to discuss so I'll look at the pen, figure out the ducks' escape route, and make repairs! I might make tiny leg shackles for them if this keeps up!"

"Moses would pick the lock. I'll take the ducks to the pond until you finish repairing the damage," Chloe said as she rounded up the five Mallards.

Eli slipped through the doors and soon had the dogs under his control.

Marty Blashfield kept his distance from Chloe and the ducks as she led them through the front entrance of Eli's workshop and studio, around the big house toward the footbridge where the newly created duck pond stood close to the creekbed.

"I really don't know how you get any work done around here," Marty leaned over the bridge railing and commented to Chloe after she'd waded into the pond and the ducks were swimming circles around her. "Seriously, Chloe. Since I've been here, those ducks and the big dog have interrupted you during meals and conversations. I'm happy to see you've broken through your creative block, but if I can be frank, sweetheart, you seem less devoted to your work."

Chloe turned so quickly, she almost lost her balance. She wrung pond water out of the hem of her sundress as she looked over at Marty standing on the bank. "Less devoted?"

"It's hard to put my finger on it exactly. You're more detached, distracted. You've always been so committed, Chloe. Almost obsessed with 'The Wilde Kingdom.'" Marty shaded his eyes from the bright August sunlight. "Maybe I'm way off the mark but I can't help wondering if you need to be more isolated from Eli Kellerman and his animals to do your best work."

"Isn't it obvious to you that Eli and his menagerie have been a part of the change in me?"

"Great. I'm happy for you, Chloe. But I arrived yesterday and we just began talking business this afternoon and that was disrupted by a flock of squawking ducks. I just want to know if you're still serious about your career as a cartoonist."

Chloe stopped wringing the skirt of her dress and let it drop, damp against her thighs. She put her hands on her hips and faced Marty squarely. "I'm damn serious, Martin Blashfield. And just to prove it, I've made a decision about the sabbatical. Go ahead and schedule the first strip—as quickly as possible. I'm ready. And I'm enough of a professional to know it."

"Good. You're making the right decision. What about the publicity?"

"I'll meet you halfway, Marty. You want me to retain a part of my old image so I won't disillusion my fans? Fine." Chloe struck her palm on the surface of the pond. "But eventually I want them to know more about the real me. Ducks, dogs, Eli Kellerman, and all!"

Inhaling deeply, Eli tried to focus his attention on the firewood stored next to the hearth in the farmhouse's enormous living room. There was a spiritual beauty to building a fire. He liked to go about the process calmly, blending the right firewood together for a consistent burn, anticipating the aroma of the more fragrant woods as he stacked them inside the fireplace.

He could hear Chloe's uneven breathing from across the room. After speaking for more than half an hour, interrupted only by his brief questions, she sat in silence on the sofa, watching as he built the fire.

The serenity he sought at the moment was elusive. As he picked up a handful of kindling, Eli watched his hand shake with the anger he was suppressing. He'd worked to create an open, honest relationship with her. Denying his feelings wasn't fair, to Chloe or to himself.

She'd waited more than two days after Marty's departure to share the particulars of the meetings they'd had during her business manager's brief stay. As she talked on the porch, her features cast in silhouette against the August twilight, the details accumulated like tinder-dry kindling.

Eli stacked the last log in the fireplace, sat down on the raised hearth, and brushed pieces of bark from his hands. He looked across the room at Chloe, sitting with her legs tucked beneath her on the sofa. Chomp lay on the floor nearby, his mournful eyes staring accusingly at Eli.

Eli struggled with his protective urges. In his eyes, she'd made a mistake. A mistake she could have prevented, had she discussed the issues with him. When could he interfere, and when did he need to stand in the shadows and watch from afar? How much was too much?

"Eli, I know my decision's upset you but—" Chloe's tone was hesitant. "Why won't you tell me what you're thinking?"

Standing, he took a match from the can on the mantel and touched it to the paper and kindling. As the fire ignited, his anger and protective urges flared.

"All right," he began. "I'll be honest. After all of our discussions about the problems publicity can create, you agree to continue being the sex symbol of cartooning." Eli tried to keep his voice level and controlled but the effort made him clench his teeth. "Publicity is publicity, Chloe." He raised his voice and clenched his fist. "How in hell could you give in so easily?"

"Marty was challenging me, Eli. He was questioning my commitment to 'The Wilde Kingdom.' He was rushing me into a decision on whether to extend my sabbatical an additional three months. Thinking back, the publicity just seemed a part of the package." Her voice cracked. He watched as she fought to gain control.

"I don't know, Eli. Maybe I was too emotional or I wasn't prepared to make any major decisions but I can't change that now. I've told you before, one of my goals is to be considered a professional in this business. I can't go back on my word."

"But can you open your eyes? You *are* a professional, Chloe." He picked up a fire iron and stabilized a large chunk of maple. "You don't have to wait for Marty or your fans or anyone else to validate that! And you have the right to change your mind."

She folded her arms across her chest and turned from him. "Not now. It's too late."

"Too late? What do you mean?"

"I left a vital piece of information out of our conversation, Eli. Marty called this afternoon while you were in the workshop." She turned back and faced him. " 'The Wilde Kingdom' starts appearing in newspapers in less than two weeks."

"Which automatically puts you—" He calculated the weeks in his head. "Behind schedule? Didn't you learn anything during your sabbatical?"

"I learned I can handle whatever comes up, Eli."

Chomp stood up and rubbed against her legs. She bent down slightly to scratch his ears. "Good dog," she said softly.

"And the publicity? When does the press corps arrive? Who gets to determine what part of your old image you're going to retain, Chloe?

Chloe stopped rubbing Chomp's ears and straightened. "Why are you so concerned about the publicity?"

"For selfish reasons. Because I want people to know the colorful, charismatic, multitalented woman

I've come to know—without the sexist hype. I guess I want everyone to know the struggle you've been through this summer. I respect and admire you, Chloe. You've worked so hard to overcome the creative block and to gain some insight into your public and private self. I'd hate to see that destroyed."

"Trust me, Eli. I've changed. I'm more aware of what I need to do to feel good about myself." She walked to the raised hearth and sat down. Staring into the fire calmed her and gave her the strength to describe her feelings. "I'm sorry if this sounds cruel, but right now, I think that means spending less time with you."

"Why? Because Marty thought you weren't obsessed with your work, is that it? You think of me as a distraction?"

"I *know* you're a distraction," she responded with a choked laugh. "I just think it'd be better for me to spend more time apart from you, to live full-time in the cottage again."

Eli sat down on the opposite side of the hearth. "Until when, Chloe?"

"A few weeks. A month. I don't know. You gave me time and space when I needed to grapple with breaking through the block, Eli." She sensed the pain her words were causing him, felt the same pain burning within her. She wasn't leaving the Kellerman farm, but she was asking for solitude. A solitude that might or might not include Eli. She wanted to make the choice herself. "Can you help me now? We've gotten so close so fast."

"Close?" Eli's blue eyes softened in the flow of firelight. "That word doesn't begin to describe it well enough. I love you, Chloe."

"Eli—no." She uttered the words without thinking, surprising herself. She put up a hand as if to ward off the meaning of the word.

"Chloe, I love you. Can you simply accept that?" Eli stared at her with unblinking eyes. "All these nights we've been together, all the tender times I've never said it aloud but I've tried to show you—"

"Stop, Eli. Please, don't. Don't hurt me."

Chapter 13

"You're a heartless brute," Chloe grumbled.

"I know." Eli continued brushing barbecue sauce on the ribs. "I'm totally heartless. Borderline criminal."

"You've set up the grill next to the footbridge on purpose."

"Why would I do a disgusting thing like that?"

"To lure me out of my cottage and into the Kellerman territory for dinner. You're not being very subtle, you know. I see the picnic basket and the blanket and the bottle of wine. You're planning a picnic in the west meadow."

"What a great idea. Come on. You've played the recluse for a week now, Chloe. I thought you might be tired of frozen entrees."

"I'm tired of you thwarting my effort at solitude

every time I turn around. I have to get ahead of schedule on the strips. The syndicate—"

"Hmm. You might want to turn around just about now. Chomp is eyeing these ribs as if he means it."

"*Champ*," she corrected. "I renamed him."

"You renamed my dog? Why?"

"Chomp sounded so—so demeaning. He's more than a set of teeth and a bottomless stomach, Eli. He's got a lot of heart and he's been sort of a champion for me. So I'm calling him Champ to sort of change his image a bit."

"Makes perfect sense. And cost-effective, too. His initials stay the same so he won't have to get new monograms for his luggage."

Chloe laughed and picked a long-stemmed daisy from the tall grasses near the footbridge. "I've really missed your sense of humor, Eli," she said quietly as she pulled a white petal from the flower's yellow center.

"Are we counting the ways we miss each other?" Eli took the daisy from her. "I miss your warmth, Chloe." He plucked a second white petal. "And your smile. The way we talk at the end of the day." With each comment, he pulled another daisy petal. "Our long walks. Swimming with the ducks. The way you understand my crazy working schedule. Making dinner together. There's a lot about you to miss." He pulled the last petal, lifted it up in the gentle evening breeze. "I miss your loving, Chloe. Or is love still a word you don't want to hear?"

He let go of the delicate white petal. Chloe watched

it float away in the wind, watched until it drifted downward toward the stream beneath the footbridge.

"Eli—" She looked back at him, saw the question in his eyes and the curve of his sculpted lips. "If I could be like that—like the petal on the wind—just floating along and accepting where the breeze takes me, maybe then I could feel comfortable with the word *love*. You have to understand, it's not something I grew up with."

"I know your life wasn't stable but there must have been people who loved you as a child and later as a teenager. You've loved people, haven't you, Chloe? You know the feeling—"

"I know the feeling and I know the pain, Eli. And I remember the two going hand in hand. Whenever I got close, something happened." She brushed her fingertips over another daisy in the tall grasses. "I no longer have the ability to float along in the wind."

"Maybe it's a matter of time." He rearranged the ribs on the grill. "I have to believe this solitude you insist on will help you in some way, but I want you to understand it's hard on me."

"I know that, Eli. It'd be so much easier to have you close so I could turn to you now. I could have used your support earlier today." She remained on the footbridge, half sitting on the rail. "I granted my first interview. By phone."

"Who got the honor?"

"A free-lance journalist in Seattle that I've had good dealings with in the past. I told her about the photos you took during the past few months and she was pretty excited about them. The two of us have a nice rapport, so I was frank about what I wanted to convey to the public."

"Would you mind being specific?"

"The main message is I don't want my private life to be quite so public anymore. I don't think I'll give art directors so much control over my image when it comes to magazine covers. And I'd like my work to speak for itself."

Eli put down the barbecue tongs and stepped onto the footbridge. "What about the sabbatical?" he asked as he drew Chloe into a loose embrace.

"I talked quite a bit about the creative block."

"Good. The public enjoys reading about a well-known personality who overcomes a crisis or a personal problem."

"I mentioned the ducks and the clay and . . ."

"And?"

"I feel that what you and I have, Eli, is private. I feel a need to protect our relationship from speculation."

"I agree for the moment. How much detail did you give this journalist when you talked about your past?"

"I was vague. I don't want people hunting in closets for my skeletons. They wouldn't find skeletons anyway. No one seemed to hang around long. I don't remember my father at all, Eli. He owned a nightclub in Los Angeles where my mother danced. And you know about my mother. She got the seven-year itch when it came to lugging a little kid around."

"A beautiful child who grew up to be a beautiful

woman with the ability to draw cows who rescue people. Who rescues you, Chloe?"

"We'll find out if the critics hate the changes in 'The Wilde Kingdom.' Lord, my life sounds like one of those made-for-TV movies. Of course, I don't have enough relatives for a miniseries."

"Who would you choose to play yourself?"

"Someone with courage to spare. I could use a little extra courage right now. 'The Wilde Kingdom' starts running in less than a week. Today's interview with Paula was the first in a series of interviews I'll be doing with different media people during the coming week. But I'm being choosy, Eli."

He ran his thumb over her bottom lip. "You've outgrown your need to be a people pleaser?"

"I still get—" She laughed as he bent to give her a teasing kiss. "—I get these occasional urges to please this one particular tall blond man who likes to picnic in meadows." She touched a finger to the silver dragon on his chest.

"And he wants to please you . . . with a picnic at sunset." Eli picked up her hand and kissed the back of her fingers. "Bend the rules a little, Ms. Wilde. And after our picnic, maybe we can find a way to bend them a lot."

"I didn't expect you so soon." Eli opened the front door of the farmhouse and let his younger brother enter. "I thought we'd be waiting until tomorrow."

"I knew it was important to Chloe so I asked for a little help from friends in Seattle. Here you go, Eli."

Gabe Kellerman dropped two armloads of newspapers and magazines on the kitchen table. "And if you'd offer me a smile and some coffee for my trouble, I'll throw in my services as a clipping service."

"I think I can meet your demands and throw in dinner." Eli poured a cup of coffee and handed it to his brother with a smile. "I didn't expect so much material. Did you bring extra copies of everything?"

"No. Chloe started getting a lot of press before 'The Wilde Kingdom' reappeared and—" Standing at the table, Gabe began sorting the pile of newspapers. "Where is she?"

"In the cottage. She's working furiously on future strips. And thinking about her future."

"Are you included in those thoughts, Eli?"

"That's a good question, Gabe, but it's one only Chloe can answer. I'm going to wake her up in the morning with breakfast in bed and the press clippings. And a very special surprise."

"Animal, vegetable, or mineral?"

"Let's just say it's one hundred percent animal, Gabe. Slightly charred."

Chloe sat on the porch swing, brushing tangles from her long dark hair and luxuriating in the haze of early-morning sunlight.

With each stroke of the brush, another lazy thought unfurled. For years, she realized, she'd sought a point of normality, a point in her life where she felt like a part of the crowd. She'd wanted to blend in, to bond with other people.

The Wilde Kingdom

Now she had to face the truth. She was unique. Her experiences and memories were like no one else's. The important thing was feeling the same emotions, sharing emotions with all humankind. Joy, happiness, hurt, pain, anger, determination . . . love.

The time away from Eli allowed her to see him in her mind's eye, away from the warmth of firelight and candlelight, stripped of the public image, simply Eli.

"Good morning," he called from the footbridge. His voice sounded unusually crisp in the cool morning air. He was carrying a tray in one hand, and a large folder in the other. "I've brought breakfast and good news. Which one do you want first?"

"Good news, of course. Let me help you." Chloe rose and cleared her drawing pad and pencils off the table by the porch railing. Eli set the tray down, then snaked an arm around her waist and kissed her gently before handing her the folder.

"Clippings from a week's worth of magazines and newspapers."

"Eli, this is frightening. I've been thinking about it but I'm not sure if I'm ready to open this up and start reading."

"Then I'll read the first few articles to you while you drink your coffee and eat your blueberry pancakes."

"Pancakes!"

"I thought food would take your mind off misery. You should feel terrific this morning. Because everyone in this state and the forty-nine others seems to think you're pretty terrific. You eat and I'll read."

For the next fifteen minutes, Chloe sipped fresh-brewed coffee and enjoyed blueberry pancakes while Eli read to her in his deep, rich, mesmerizing voice. She recalled the web of intimacy he had created with his voice in the top of an oak tree the day they met.

Eli stopped reading and stared at her for several moments.

"What is it?" she asked. "You haven't come across a negative comment yet."

"It's not that, Chloe. I just wanted you to know that you're not the only one who's been changed these past few months."

"I know that, Eli. I've watched you loosen up and I don't know where that snob went, but he hasn't been seen around here for weeks."

"I was never a real snob."

"Borderline snob."

"Okay, borderline but endearing."

"Agreed." She laughed and lay back against the cushions in the porch swing. She grew serious. "Actually, I saw something in your workshop last week that interested me. You put a ladybug on a leaf. you never do insects or creatures of any kind. Why the change?"

"It was time to challenge myself. A leaf standing alone commands attention but a leaf with a ladybug or a treefrog on it is a habitat. It becomes more dimensional in purpose."

"So you're going to join me in the animal kingdom?"

"I already have, Chloe. Look closely at your breakfast tray."

"I don't see anything."

"Under the second napkin."

She lifted the second napkin. There stood a small silver replica of Bar-B-Cue the Cow. Tastefully styled as only Eli could do, but with a whimsy he never displayed in his other works. She picked up the silver Holstein and studied the detail. Tears came to her eyes and she fought to swallow the ache in her throat.

"Eli—I can't find the words. I should say—*the word*." As she embraced him, a sob tore from her throat. "It's time for me to face the truth, to take the chance. I love you, Eli." She kissed the edge of his mouth. "I love the public Kellerman and I love the private Kellerman and the man who makes me blueberry pancakes even though I've been hiding away from him, a man who brings me silver cows on a breakfast tray—"

"Chloe—"

"A man who makes me feel safe even when I'm alone because you've helped me find my own strength, Eli."

"You've helped me find my sense of humor again, Reverend Wilde. You and your crazy flock of ducks and your cartoon characters. I want you to be with me forever, Chloe."

"Forever sounds like a long, long time, Eli. It sounds wonderful."

"You don't need to go looking for extra courage, brave lady. I love you."

From the <u>New York Times</u> bestselling author of <u>Morning Glory</u>

LaVyrle Spencer

One of today's best-loved authors of bittersweet human drama and captivating romance.

___	SPRING FANCY (On sale Sept. '89)	0-515-10122-2/$3.95
___	YEARS	0-515-08489-1/$4.95
___	SEPARATE BEDS	0-515-09037-9/$4.95
___	HUMMINGBIRD	0-515-09160-X/$4.95
___	A HEART SPEAKS	0-515-09039-5/$4.50
___	THE GAMBLE	0-515-08901-X/$4.95
___	VOWS	0-515-09477-3/$4.95
___	THE HELLION	0-515-09951-1/$4.50

<u>Check book(s). Fill out coupon. Send to:</u>

BERKLEY PUBLISHING GROUP
390 Murray Hill Pkwy., Dept. B
East Rutherford, NJ 07073

NAME_____

ADDRESS_____

CITY_____

STATE_____ZIP_____

**PLEASE ALLOW 6 WEEKS FOR DELIVERY.
PRICES ARE SUBJECT TO CHANGE
WITHOUT NOTICE.**

POSTAGE AND HANDLING:
$1.00 for one book, 25¢ for each additional. Do not exceed $3.50.

BOOK TOTAL	$____
POSTAGE & HANDLING	$____
APPLICABLE SALES TAX (CA, NJ, NY, PA)	$____
TOTAL AMOUNT DUE	$____

PAYABLE IN US FUNDS.
(No cash orders accepted.)

NORMA BEISHIR'S

ANGELS AT MIDNIGHT

ASHLEY HOLLISTER--Her world fell apart when she lost custody of her only child... COLLIN DEVERELL--His vast inheritance was all but destroyed... Together, Ashley and Collin vowed to reclaim what was rightfully theirs--driven by a common passion to defeat their enemies.

DANCE OF THE GODS

"... has got it all! Mystery and megabucks, thrills and chills, sex and romance. This is a runaway rollercoaster ride which grips you from page one and races to its explosive climax!"

--Judith Gould, Bestselling author of SINS

_ANGELS AT MIDNIGHT 0-425-11406-6/$4.50
_DANCE OF THE GODS 0-425-10839-2/$4.50

Check book(s). Fill out coupon. Send to:

BERKLEY PUBLISHING GROUP
390 Murray Hill Pkwy., Dept. B
East Rutherford, NJ 07073

NAME_____
ADDRESS_____
CITY_____
STATE_____ ZIP_____

PLEASE ALLOW 6 WEEKS FOR DELIVERY.
PRICES ARE SUBJECT TO CHANGE
WITHOUT NOTICE.

POSTAGE AND HANDLING:
$1.00 for one book, 25¢ for each additional. Do not exceed $3.50.

BOOK TOTAL $____
POSTAGE & HANDLING $____
APPLICABLE SALES TAX $____
(CA, NJ, NY, PA)
TOTAL AMOUNT DUE $____

PAYABLE IN US FUNDS.
(No cash orders accepted.)

New York Times **bestselling author of**
The Accidental Tourist **and** *Breathing Lessons*

ANNE TYLER

"To read a novel by Anne Tyler is to fall in love!" —*People Magazine*

Anne Tyler's novels are a rare mixture of laughter and tears. Critics have praised her fine gift for characterization and her skill at blending touching insight and powerful emotions to create superb entertainment.

___Dinner at the Homesick Restaurant	0-425-09868-0/$4.95
___The Tin Can Tree	0-425-09903-2/$3.95
___Morgan's Passing	0-425-09872-9/$4.50
___Searching for Caleb	0-425-09876-1/$4.50
___If Morning Ever Comes	0-425-09883-4/$3.95
___The Clock Winder	0-425-09902-4/$4.50
___A Slipping-Down Life	0-425-10362-5/$4.50
___Celestial Navigation	0-425-09840-0/$3.95
___Earthly Possessions	0-425-10167-3/$3.95
___The Accidental Tourist	0-425-11423-6/$4.95

Check book(s). Fill out coupon. Send to:

BERKLEY PUBLISHING GROUP
390 Murray Hill Pkwy., Dept. B
East Rutherford, NJ 07073

NAME_____

ADDRESS_____

CITY_____

STATE_____ZIP_____

PLEASE ALLOW 6 WEEKS FOR DELIVERY.
PRICES ARE SUBJECT TO CHANGE
WITHOUT NOTICE.

POSTAGE AND HANDLING:
$1.00 for one book, 25¢ for each additional. Do not exceed $3.50.

BOOK TOTAL	$____
POSTAGE & HANDLING	$____
APPLICABLE SALES TAX (CA, NJ, NY, PA)	$____
TOTAL AMOUNT DUE	$____

PAYABLE IN US FUNDS.
(No cash orders accepted.)

The phenomenal national
bestseller from the author of
The Accidental Tourist!

ANNE TYLER
Breathing Lessons

**WINNER OF THE 1989
PULITZER PRIZE**

Everyone knows an ordinary couple like the Morans, and the Morans think they know themselves. But on the road to a friend's funeral they discover just how extraordinary their ordinary lives really are....

"She is at the top of her powers."

—*New York Times Book Review*

"Humor is woven into almost every sentence."

—*USA Today*

__Breathing Lessons (On sale Oct. '89)   0-425-11774-X/$5.50

Check book(s). Fill out coupon. Send to:

BERKLEY PUBLISHING GROUP
390 Murray Hill Pkwy., Dept. B
East Rutherford, NJ 07073

NAME_____
ADDRESS_____
CITY_____
STATE_____ZIP_____

**PLEASE ALLOW 6 WEEKS FOR DELIVERY.
PRICES ARE SUBJECT TO CHANGE
WITHOUT NOTICE.**

POSTAGE AND HANDLING:
$1.00 for one book, 25¢ for each additional. Do not exceed $3.50.

BOOK TOTAL $____

POSTAGE & HANDLING $____

APPLICABLE SALES TAX $____
(CA, NJ, NY, PA)

TOTAL AMOUNT DUE $____

PAYABLE IN US FUNDS.
(No cash orders accepted.)